THE IMPOSSIBLE QUEST

TO MY DARLING ELLA, THE ORIGINAL
LADY ELANOR x

First American Edition 2016
Kane Miller, A Division of EDC Publishing

Text copyright © Kate Forsyth 2015

First published by Scholastic Press, a division of Scholastic Australia Pty Limited in 2015.
Cover illustration and map on page iv by Jeremy Reston.
Logo design by blacksheep-uk.com.
Internal photography: brick texture on page i © GiorgioMagini|istockphoto.com; castle
on page ii and folios © ivan-96|istockphoto.com.
This edition published under license from Scholastic Australia Pty Limited.
All rights reserved, including the rights of reproduction in whole or in part in any form.

For information contact:
Kane Miller, A Division of EDC Publishing
P.O. Box 470663
Tulsa, OK 74147-0663
www.kanemiller.com
www.edcpub.com
www.usbornebooksandmore.com

Library of Congress Control Number: 2015945352

Printed and bound in the United States of America
10 11 12 13 14 15 16 17 18 19

ISBN: 978-1-61067-418-8

KATE FORSYTH

THE IMPOSSIBLE QUEST

5

BATTLE OF THE HEROES

Kane Miller
A DIVISION OF EDC PUBLISHING

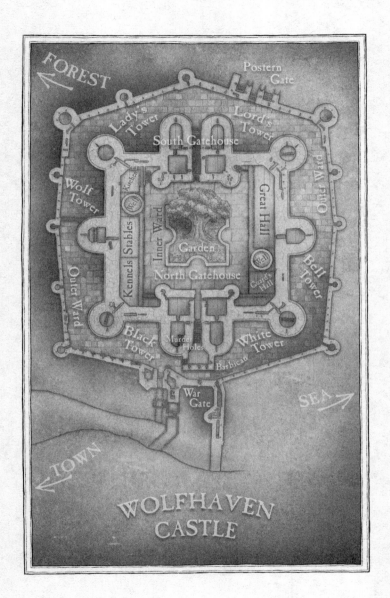

FOREST

Postern Gate

Lady's Tower

Lord's Tower

South Gatehouse

Wolf Tower

Kitchen

Well

Great Hall

Outer Ward

Kennels Stables

Inner Ward

Garden

North Gatehouse

Well

Guard Hall

Bell Tower

Outer Ward

Black Tower

Murder Holes

White Tower

Barbican

War Gate

SEA

TOWN

WOLFHAVEN CASTLE

1

TENTACLES FROM THE DEEP

A wild storm raged around the Lost Isles. Lightning stabbed down, splitting the darkness apart.

A small boat painted with the eyes of an owl pitched up and down on the waves. Dark shapes crouched below the thrashing sail.

Flash. A girl in rags of white gripping the tiller.

Flash. A boy kneeling by the side of a huge dog howling at the storm.

Flash. A girl fighting to calm a rearing unicorn.

Flash. A boy in a torn cloak hauling at a rope, a small dragon with spread wings on his shoulder.

Darkness fell again. Nothing could be seen but the flying tatters of foam, the white-crested surge of a wave. Hail clattered on the wooden deck.

The sea began to swirl. The boat spun as helplessly as a leaf in an eddy. A great whirlpool formed, lit by flashes of green fire. The boat whirled around its outer curve, sucked towards the vortex.

The sail tore free and was whipped away by the wind. The boat plunged, spray crashing over the hull.

A giant tentacle writhed up out of the churning water and wrapped around the tiny craft. Timbers groaned and cracked. Another tentacle snaked up, then another. The mast smashed down. Dark shapes tumbled into the white froth.

Then Owl-Eyes was dragged into the immense beaked mouth that lurked in the depths of the whirlpool.

In an old stone cottage on Adderwell Island, four children knelt around a large obsidian ball set on golden claws. Within the smoky darkness of the ball, they watched the boat being torn apart and swallowed down by the monster in the ocean's depths.

"Lucky we weren't on board." Sebastian felt sick and shaken.

"Do you think it'll work? Do you think they'll believe we're dead?" Elanor asked.

"I hope so," Tom said fervently.

Quinn hurriedly draped a cloth over the obsidian ball. She did not want anyone to know they were using the witch's ball to spy beyond the Lost Isles. "Those witches may still suspect a trick. We'll need to remain as stealthy and secretive as we can."

Outside, the rain began to ease. Quinn's tense white face relaxed. "That's a good sign! If the storm lessens, we can try and get away from here."

The witch sisters, Lady Mortlake and Mistress Mauldred, had summoned the tempest in their rage at the death of their mother, Githa, and it had kept the four friends marooned on the Lost Isles for days. At times, the storm had been so violent they had feared the witches sought to submerge the Lost Isles, just as the rest of the kingdom had been drowned nearly thirty years earlier. Willowmere had been torn to pieces and half drowned in the stormy gale, and so the children and their beasts had taken refuge in Githa's cottage so they were not an added burden on the people of the isles.

"They're trying to kill us," Elanor had gasped, after one particularly wild night in which it seemed the old cottage would be wrenched from its foundations and carried away by the wind.

"Let's make those witch sisters think they have succeeded, then," Tom had said.

So the people of the Lost Isles had woven four life-sized figures from willow twigs. They had also made a unicorn, a baby dragon and a dog, all from the same wicker as their basket boats. With the figures arranged on board to look as real as possible, Owl-Eyes had been sent out into the stormy sea under the propulsion of magic. The children had not expected their boat to be devoured by a sea monster, but now hoped their trick had worked and the witches truly believed them to be dead.

"We've lost too much time," Quinn said. "We

have to get back to Wolfhaven as fast as possible. I think we should leave now—if we can . . ."

Everybody nodded, not quite looking at her.

None of us know how to behave around Quinn anymore, Sebastian thought. It was so strange to think the raggedy witch girl they'd been traveling with was really a queen.

Quinn had always believed she'd been abandoned by her parents as a baby. Thirteen years earlier, she had been found bobbing around on the ocean's waves in a basket, and had been taken in by Arwen, the Grand Teller of Wolfhaven Castle, who had raised her to learn the witch's craft.

Yet here on the Lost Isles, Quinn had discovered the truth of how she came to be forsaken in that floating basket. Her father had been King Conway of Stormness. He and his queen, her mother, had drowned in a shipwreck by this very island. A tiny baby, Quinn had been saved by the people of the Lost Isles and put to sea in one of the little coracles woven from willow twigs. The basket boat had bobbed its way across the ocean to safety at Wolfhaven Castle, with nobody realizing that the baby tucked inside was the daughter of the drowned king.

Now Quinn's great-uncle Ivor was King of Stormness, not knowing that she—the true queen—had survived the wreck.

"What, no arguments? What's wrong with you all?" Quinn demanded.

"Nothing," Elanor said, after a little pause, then added hesitantly, "your Grace."

"Oh, go boil your heads!" Quinn cried. "So my father was the king! *I'm* still exactly the same. It doesn't change anything."

"It *does* change things," Sebastian insisted. "It changes everything."

Quinn shook her head stubbornly. "No, it doesn't. I have no proof anyway—only a silver baby's rattle and an old man's story. Do you think King Ivor will surrender his throne to me with that proof alone? Do you think I *want* him to?"

"But you have the right." Sebastian was puzzled.

"It seems to me that all the recent kings of Stormness have met with an untimely end," Quinn said. "I have no desire to be the next to die."

"That was because of Githa's evil plots," Tom pointed out. "But you defeated her. She's dead now."

"Her daughters are still alive and they have taken over our castle and imprisoned our friends and families," Quinn answered. "And don't forget—they just did their very best to kill us too."

"It just feels weird," Tom said. "I mean . . . knowing you really are—"

"I'm Quinn," she pleaded. "As I ever was."

He gave a crooked smile. "Very well, then, Quinn, what do you think we should do now?"

"Let's look in the obsidian ball again and see what is happening at Wolfhaven Castle," she suggested. "We must be very careful, though. We don't want the witches to realize we're watching."

The four friends held hands again, and Quinn carefully cast aside the covering cloth. Looking down into the swirling darkness of the ball, she chanted:

"MAGIC BALL, BLACK AS NIGHT,
SHOW US THE CASTLE HEIGHT,

A̲n̲d̲ ̲t̲h̲e̲ ̲e̲n̲e̲m̲i̲e̲s̲ ̲w̲e̲ ̲w̲i̲s̲h̲ ̲t̲o̲ ̲s̲m̲i̲t̲e̲,

K̲e̲e̲p̲ ̲u̲s̲ ̲h̲i̲d̲d̲e̲n̲ ̲f̲r̲o̲m̲ ̲t̲h̲e̲i̲r̲ ̲s̲i̲g̲h̲t̲."

Sebastian saw the dark mist part within the ball. Wolfhaven Castle stood on its stony outcrop, black-armored knights marching along the battlements. More knights practiced with sword and spear in the outer ward. Lord Mortlake stood watching, his helmet with its boar tusks tucked in the crook of his elbow. Rank after rank of bog-men stood at attention behind him, staring sightlessly ahead.

A giant boar thundered across the lawn, its hooves tearing up the grass. Lady Mortlake rode on its back, her black hair streaming behind her. She drew the great tusked pig up to a snorting halt beside her husband. "We've done it! Those wretched children have all drowned!"

"What of their beasts?" her husband snapped. "You know I want the unicorn for its healing horn and the dragon's teeth so I can conjure up another army of bog-men." He gestured towards the rows and rows of bony, leathery creatures standing so still behind him.

"And that griffin would be of use, too!"

Lady Mortlake slid off the boar and reached out one hand to stroke her husband's cheek. "We could not kill the children without killing their beasts, my love, you know that." As his anger flared, she soothed him. "You don't need the beasts anymore! You are the only heir to the throne now that Lady Elanor and that other troublesome girl are dead. All we need to do now is kill the king."

A cruel smile curved Lord Mortlake's lips. "You are right! But can it be done? Your mother failed at the crucial moment."

"Of course it can!" Lady Mortlake replied. "My sister and I shall cast another spell at sunset on the night of the dark moon. That is only three days away. Our only problem is . . . we shall need blood."

"We have a dungeon full of prisoners," he answered indifferently. "Use their blood."

Lady Mortlake smiled. "As always, you are full of wisdom, my lord. We'll make a spell of such power that we can strike down the king from afar." She vaulted back onto the giant boar and wheeled the beast around. "I shall go and tell my sister! She wants to kill them all now. I will tell her to wait till the moon is dark before she takes her revenge."

As the boar bounded away, the vision slowly dimmed and faded. Quinn swiftly flung the cloth over the obsidian ball once more, making sure that no one could use it to spy on them.

Sebastian sat back on his heels, looking around at the white faces of his friends. "They plan to murder them all! For a spell to kill the king!"

"We have to get back fast!" Quinn cried. "The moon is waning now. We only have a couple of nights till the moon is dark . . . before they'll all be dead."

She jumped up and began to pace back and forth, her ragged white skirt fluttering around her bare feet. Fergus the wolfhound gazed at her with anxious eyes, whining. He didn't like being in the witch's cottage, even though the people of Willowmere had scrubbed it from floor to ceiling. A strange smell still clung to its stones, making all of the magical beasts uneasy. Quickthorn the unicorn stamped his great hoof, a rim of white showing around his dark eyes, while the griffin, Rex, lashed his lion's tail. Beltaine the baby dragon was perched high up in the smoke-blackened rafters, her blue eyes slitted, spitting out a shower of fiery sparks. The wolf cub Wulfric was pressed, shivering, against the wolfhound's shaggy side, while Fergus's tail was tucked between his legs.

"Without Owl-Eyes," Elanor said, "how on earth are we to get home?"

"We'll go in coracles, just like Quinn did when she was a baby," Tom suggested.

"All that way, in a tiny little basket boat?" Sebastian cried.

"If Quinn could do it as a helpless baby, we can do it now," Tom said.

"But what about the beasts?" Sebastian asked.

"Ela and Quickthorn can fit into one coracle," Tom said. "I'll go in another with Rex. He can fly most of the time and just come down to the boat when he grows tired. Sebastian, you go in another coracle with Bel, and Quinn can take Fergus and Wulfric in hers."

"It'll take us forever to paddle all that way," Sebastian groaned.

"Not if I ask the sea serpent to tow us," Quinn said.

The others stared at her in amazement. "Do . . . do you think that's wise?" Tom asked.

"Why not?" Quinn scowled at him.

"Well, he's just such a dangerous creature . . ."

"I saved his life," Quinn said, gesturing towards the sea serpent scale resting against the wall. Large and round like a shield, it had been cut from the breast of the sea serpent by Githa. But Quinn had healed the wound with water enchanted by Quickthorn's horn and stopped the great beast's lifeblood from ebbing away. "I'm sure he will tow us if I ask."

"I'm not being towed along by that thing!" Sebastian declared. He turned to Tom and Elanor. "You should have seen the sea serpent kill the witch! I'll have nightmares for years."

"*I'm* the one who got bitten," Tom said. "You think *I* want to go anywhere near a monster like that again?"

"It's the only way to get back to Wolfhaven in time," Quinn insisted.

Sebastian thought of the poor people of Wolfhaven Castle, imprisoned in the dungeons and now threatened with death. It had been three weeks since the castle had fallen to Lord Mortlake's sinister forces. In that time, Sebastian and his friends had been on the run, battling all kinds of dangerous monsters and wicked enemies. Somehow they had survived. Now it was time to fulfill the last part of their quest. He and his friends had to find the sleeping heroes under the castle, awaken them and beg them to help save the castle and rescue the prisoners.

He remembered the prophecy that had set them out on this impossible quest in the first place:

WHEN THE WOLF LIES DOWN WITH THE WOLFHOUND,
AND THE STONES OF THE CASTLE SING,
THE SLEEPING HEROES SHALL WAKE FOR THE CROWN,
AND THE BELLS OF VICTORY RING.

GRIFFIN FEATHER AND UNICORN'S HORN,
SEA SERPENT SCALE AND DRAGON'S TOOTH,
BRING THEM TOGETHER AT FIRST LIGHT OF DAWN,
AND YOU SHALL SEE THIS SPELL'S TRUTH.

It had seemed an unattainable goal, but the four friends had achieved such incredible things in the last three weeks. Could they somehow manage this final challenge?

Sebastian squared his shoulders. "All right. We'll have to risk it."

"And once we get there, we'll need to slip back into Wolfhaven Castle without those witches seeing us," Quinn said, biting her thumbnail.

"We could try at night," Sebastian said. "That creepy mist will help hide us. But Lord Mortlake's knights will be guarding the castle gate. It'll be impossible to get in that way."

"Well, we need to get into the caves under the castle," Quinn said, "so we can awaken the sleeping heroes. The best way would be to go back through the secret water gate under the bridge."

"So that means we need to paddle the coracles through the harbor mouth and all the way to the bridge . . . right under the enemy's nose," Elanor said, her forehead creased in thought. "It'll be dangerous."

"We'll just have to hope the mist and the darkness

hide us," Quinn said. "And somehow keep our wits while we're in it. We'll need to find those sleeping heroes fast and give them our gifts!"

"Beltaine is losing her baby teeth," Sebastian said, looking affectionately at the little dragon. He held up a small tooth, shining bone white and as sharp as a dagger. "I got this one from her this morning."

"So we have all four of the magical ingredients now!" Quinn lifted up the translucent sea serpent scale so the firelight glowed through it. "Let's go find the sleeping heroes!"

2

»——SEA SERPENT——«

T om stared out across the lagoon to the churning
ocean. It was still dark and wild, but the sky
overhead was a delicate blue.

"I will call the sea serpent and see if he comes."
Quinn hurried down the steep path towards the
lagoon, the others following behind.

Tom couldn't help hoping that the sea serpent
wouldn't heed her call. He would never forget the
terrifying moment when his foot had been pierced
by a sea serpent's fang. It had been like one of those
nightmares when time slowed and matter became
so heavy that nothing could shift it. The memory of
stumbling into the shadowy vale of death shot a cold

bolt down his spine.

Elanor turned and waited for him, whispering, "Are you all right? Does your foot hurt?"

Tom shook his head. His foot had healed, but he feared it would take longer for his spirit to follow.

I just have to stop thinking about it, he told himself.

Then he heard Quinn calling. "Sea serpent, are you there? Do you hear me?"

She stood on a rock, arms stretched out, her staff in one hand. Her wild black curls flew in the wind. Sebastian was close behind her; Tom and Elanor stood on the path above.

Tom saw a long, dark, slender shape writhing swiftly through the water. His legs wobbled. He found it hard to catch a breath.

"Do not fear," Elanor whispered, taking his arm. "He's our friend." But her voice was shaking so much she could hardly speak.

The sea serpent burst from the water. His red eyes gazed down, unblinking, at Quinn. His long body, silver scales striped with black, coiled and twisted below him, deep into the water.

Sebastian rushed forward, trying his best to protect Quinn from an attack, but the snake did not strike. Instead, he bowed low before Quinn.

"I knew you would come," Quinn said gently. "Will you help us?"

The sea serpent bowed his head once more, his body coiling and uncoiling beneath him.

"Then come back here to us at sunset." Quinn pointed to the sun and then to where it would set in the west. "I shall expect you."

The sea serpent slithered back into the water.

Elanor sat down abruptly. "I thought you were done for, Quinn!"

"I knew he would not hurt me," Quinn answered serenely. "I saved his life."

Four coracles raced along through the dark waters, tied together by a long rope to the neck of the sea serpent. A white wake of foam arrowed behind them.

"We're going really fast," Tom called to the others.

"Is it long till dawn?" Elanor's voice was so faint it was hard to hear her. "It's scary racing through the darkness. I can't see the waves before they hit us."

"Not long," Quinn called back. "Look, there's a little line of light to the east."

The coracles bounced from wave to wave, making Tom's stomach drop sickeningly each time. It seemed impossible that the four tiny boats could stay afloat in these wild and treacherous waters. Woven simply from willow twigs interlaced together and covered with snakeskin, the coracles were so light that they could each be lifted and carried by a single person. Tom gripped the wicker rim as tightly as he could.

Slowly the line of light along the eastern horizon spread. The sea serpent's head and sinuous neck were silhouetted against the silvery-pink sky.

"Are you . . . are you sure that thing is safe?" Tom called to Quinn.

"Don't call him a 'thing'!" she retorted at once. "He's a perfectly beautiful sea serpent. And he's not safe, of course he's not. He's wild and magical and dangerous, just like your griffin. But right now, he's helping us. We can't get to Wolfhaven without him."

Tom gazed upward. He hoped Rex was safe up there. As if in response to his thoughts, he heard the griffin's high shriek, far above him, and saw his dark winged shape swoop past.

"Are you sure we're still headed east?" Tom heard his voice shake. "The serpent could be planning on taking us far out to sea and abandoning us there."

"Toad spit! If he wanted to kill us, he would have done so already," Quinn snapped back. "I tell you, he's our friend. And without him, we'd have had to paddle all this way. You should be grateful."

Tom bit back a wry grin. It was easy to forget that Quinn was really a queen when she was so cranky.

"Well, if he's your pet now, you'd better find a name for him," he called to her.

Quinn laughed, startled. "I don't think he's really a pet. But yes, we should give him a name. It sounds rude to just call him 'him' all the time."

"How do you know he's a 'he'?" Elanor shouted.

"He has the markings of an adder," Quinn called

back. "I suspect the sea serpents were adders which were transformed into giants by Githa's magic. Then when the kingdom drowned . . . well, they adapted. Anyway, he's silver. Female adders are brown."

"You could be right. The islanders did call the witch's island Adderwell." Sebastian cupped his hands around his mouth to shout back.

"Of course I'm right. I'm always right."

"Yes, your Grace, of course, your Grace," he hollered mockingly.

"Don't call me that!"

"Sorry." Sebastian grinned at Quinn. "Well then, what are you going to call your sweet little pet? Slayer?"

"No!"

"How about Slinky?" Tom teased her.

"No."

"Sir Hiss?" Elanor suggested.

"He does look like a knight in his silver chain mail," Quinn said.

"And he has a pair of very sharp swords." Tom looked down at his foot, and flexed it gently.

"Or sabers . . . that's what I'll call him. Sabre."

"It's a perfect name," Elanor said.

The newly named sea serpent sped straight as an arrow, and the sun swung over their heads and then began to sink down into the west. The children were glad of their waterskins and the food that the islanders had given them. Beltaine swooped down to perch on the edge of Sebastian's coracle, almost capsizing it. Little sparks blew in and out of her flared nostrils, and Sebastian had to quickly stamp out a few that landed on the wicker.

The sea glittered golden, then orange and then slowly turned an intense violet blue as the sun sank.

The four friends sat in their tiny basket boats, staring out into the night. Quickthorn was curled uncomfortably in the bottom of the coracle. Elanor rested her back against him. He was warm and strong, and smelled of the forest, of damp leaves and wild sorrel. Comforted, Elanor drifted off to sleep. She woke in the early hours of the morning, to see the thin moon rising in the sky. Ahead were dark peaks, piled high like clouds. "Look! Land!" she cried.

3

QUICKTHORN

The towering cliffs gradually gentled to the softly rolling hills of Wolfhaven. Green meadows were divided into patchwork squares by hedges of hawthorn, elder and cherry plum.

All around the coracles, the sea heaved and rolled. Elanor twined her fingers in Quickthorn's tangled black mane. The unicorn was restless, and Elanor's touch calmed him. Elanor felt anxious about the task that lay ahead of them. It all seemed so impossible. Even if they did manage to raise the four sleeping heroes, how were they meant to stand against the might of Lord Mortlake and the bog-men, and the dark magic of Lady Mortlake and Mistress Mauldred?

Quickthorn whickered and nudged her shoulder with his velvety nose. Elanor smiled a little shakily and dug in her pack for a small, wizened apple. The unicorn chomped it down greedily. Elanor wrapped her arms around his neck and buried her face in his mane. "I hope you stay with me always," she whispered.

Quickthorn neighed softly. A lump came into Elanor's throat. She knew she could not keep the unicorn forever. He was a wild creature of the woods, not meant for saddle and bridle. The closer they came to Wolfhaven, the closer came the time of their parting . . . Elanor felt she couldn't bear it.

As the sun passed overhead and began to sink towards the west, Quickthorn became restless. "We need to go ashore," Elanor said.

"We can't head into Wolfhaven Harbor until it's dark, anyway," Tom said. "Let's go ashore and gather some food and have a rest before we tackle the next part of our quest."

Eventually Quinn saw a small, rocky bay where they could splash ashore and drag the coracles up onto the pebbly beach.

A narrow track led up into a wood where the sun fell, dappled, through the green leaves of oak. Quickthorn began to munch grass hungrily and the children drank from a small spring. Fergus and Wulfric drank too, the wolf cub crouched between the wolfhound's shaggy paws. Rex took roost on a rock shelf, wings folded back along his lion haunches.

"I'll set some snares and see if I can catch us something for supper." Tom dug around in his pockets for some string.

"I'll gather some herbs," Quinn said. "My pouch is practically empty."

Elanor found an apple tree and filled the tattered skirts of her dress. Sebastian gathered an armful of firewood and built a fireplace from stones. The dragon gamboled at his feet, smoke puffing around her head.

"Quinn, can I borrow your dagger to cut some branches?" he asked. "How I loathe being without my sword!"

"Sure," Quinn answered, passing him the long silver dagger she wore in a sheath buckled to her belt. Then, as Sebastian went to hack at a small, crooked tree beside the spring, she cried, "Not that one! You can't cut that tree."

Sebastian turned to stare at her. "How come?"

"It is an elder tree. It's the worst of bad luck to cut branches from an elder."

Sebastian paused. "Don't tell me. It's a magic tree." He rolled his eyes at Elanor, who smiled. Quinn was funny about trees.

"It is one of the most magic trees of all," Quinn answered seriously. "Elder trees are sacred to the Lady. Arwen says it is a threshold tree, and so is a kind of gateway between worlds. It's said that a flute made from elder, like Tom's, will call the faery folk to you."

"Really?" Tom looked up from his snare making.

Elanor examined the tree. It was old, gnarled and mossy, but not very tall. Delicate clusters of black berries hung below serrated green leaves.

"*Elder is the Lady's Tree, burn it not or cursed you'll be*," Quinn chanted, then added in a very different tone of voice, "the berries are delicious cooked with apples and honey."

"Then I'll cook some for us," Tom said, reaching

out to pluck a branch. Then he paused. "Shall I be cursed if I pick the berries?"

"Not if you ask nicely," Quinn replied. She bowed to the crooked little tree. "Dear lady of the elder tree, please bless us with your bounty."

Quinn picked several heavy sprays of berries and passed them to Tom, who washed them in the spring, then set them to steep in water. She then took one of the apples and laid it among the knobbly roots. "In payment," she told Elanor. "One should never take from the Lady without giving something in return."

Elanor was searching for mushrooms when she heard Sebastian call. "Come and see!"

She hurried up the track and onto a high headland. Sebastian stood, shading his eyes with his hand as he stared to the south. Elanor joined him, with Quinn and Tom coming up behind. They all stared where Sebastian pointed.

Wolfhaven Castle stood on its hill, wrapped in thick mist.

"We're almost home," Elanor breathed. Quinn put her arm around her shoulders.

"At least we know for sure that the magical mist is still there," Tom said. "What those witches spun to conceal the castle from the eyes of others will work to conceal us from them."

"I feel so sorry for everyone in the town," Quinn said. "Living in that suffocating fog all this time."

"Tomorrow . . ." Elanor said. "Tomorrow, the sun will shine on Wolfhaven again."

No one dared say what they were truly thinking. Elanor smiled with an effort. "Come on, then. Staring at the mist won't make it go away."

Subdued, the four friends made their way back down to the clearing. The sun was slanting in long lines through the trees. "Let's eat and rest a little," Tom said. "It's going to be a long night."

Tom had managed to snare two fat wood pigeons and he set them to roast over the fire, then sliced the mushrooms and tossed them into a pan with wild garlic and butter, which the people of the Lost Isles had given them. In another small pot, Tom set the elderberries to simmer with apples and honey. While it all cooked, the children sharpened their weapons.

"Supper's almost ready," Tom said. He doled out the mushrooms and wild garlic, and used his dagger to carve up the roasted pigeons. Fergus and Wulfric sat very close to him, staring at him with imploring dark eyes, and he tossed them some of the meat.

"This is so delicious," Quinn said, eating hungrily. "The best meal we've had in weeks!"

"Tom is the best cook," Sebastian said.

A shadow crossed Tom's face. "No, that's my mam."

"Well, one day you'll be the castle cook and everyone will say you're the best cook in the land!"

The shadow on Tom's face deepened.

"It really is good, Tom," Elanor said. "Thank you."

"It's the butter," he answered shortly, and got up to wash his plate in the spring.

Elanor rose to do the same. As she bent, her hands in the cold water, she heard a faint rustling from the tree nearby.

She looked around sharply. The elder tree stood, hunched and still in the shadows. Elanor bent to the spring again, and then noticed something strange.

The apple left in the gnarled roots was gone.

When the western sky was red and a single star shone in the violet-blue east, Elanor said, "It's time to go."

"We'd better make our final plans," Tom said. "We'll take only what's necessary."

"We'll need weapons," Sebastian said. "If only I had my sword!"

Elanor took the long, black unicorn's horn from her pack. "I'll need this."

"And I'll need Bel's tooth." Sebastian took out the curved dragon's tooth, sharp as an ivory blade.

Quinn picked up the sea serpent's scale, as big and round as a silver shield.

Tom flourished a handful of golden griffin feathers. "Every time Rex dropped a feather, I picked it up," he said. "Just to make sure."

"So all we have to do now is get into the caves under the castle and find those sleeping heroes," Elanor said, pretending she felt brave and certain.

"We'll wait till it's fully dark," Tom said. "Under the cover of all that mist, we can slip into the harbor and find the secret entrance under the bridge."

"How will we stop the mist from making us sick and stupid?" Quinn asked.

"Let's tie a cloth over our mouths and noses," Tom suggested. "And keep an eye on each other. If anyone looks like they're getting drowsy, we'll have to shake them awake."

"We'll need to be as quiet as possible. The harbor and the town will be well guarded by those bog-men," Sebastian said.

"If we sneak into the harbor around midnight, that'll give us the rest of the night to find the sleeping heroes, if we have to awaken them at dawn," Elanor said. "I hope that's enough time."

"Sure it is," Sebastian replied with gusto, wrapping his cloak around him and securing it with the brooch Arwen had given him at the beginning of their adventures. The carved wooden dragon had once held a lump of amber in its claws, which had proved to be a dragon's egg. The dragon within had hatched in the Beast of Blackmoor Bog's fire and now lay curled beside Sebastian, tendrils of smoke rising lazily from her nostrils. Sebastian had rescued his brooch from the flames. It had been charred black, but it still did its job securing Sebastian's cloak . . . and he could not bear to part with it.

"What are we going to do with the beasts?" Elanor asked. "We can't take them into the caves with us."

Everyone looked at her in sudden realization.

"I guess I'll have to say good-bye to Sabre," Quinn said, looking down to where the weary sea serpent rested in the bay. She looked sad. "But I'll ask him to tow us to the mouth of the harbor first."

"Well, I always knew Rex couldn't come into the caves with us," Tom said. "But he'll find somewhere to roost overnight. I think we'll need him in the battle, once we've woken the heroes."

"I'm taking Beltaine," Sebastian said stubbornly. "I'm not leaving her behind."

"I don't think she'll like the caves," Elanor said. "They're so cold and dark and cramped. She won't be able to fly around very easily."

"She won't want to leave me." Sebastian scratched the baby dragon under the chin, and Beltaine slitted her eyes and purred deep in her throat, smoke puffing from her nostrils.

Elanor looked over to the shadowy trees. "Well, I can't take Quickthorn into the caves."

"Yes," Quinn said, after a long pause. "You'll have to leave him here. You're right. He's not made for caves."

Elanor pressed both hands against her eyes and swallowed hard. "Do you think he'll be safe?"

"He can protect himself," Sebastian said staunchly. "Don't worry."

In silence, the group made the last of their preparations. The shadows deepened.

"We need to get going," Quinn said.

"Let's just say good-bye to Quickthorn," Elanor said. The unicorn lifted his head and blew gently through his nostrils. The four children stood around him, stroking his velvety coat.

"You've been such a faithful friend. Thank you," Elanor whispered. She had a hard lump in her throat.

Quickthorn put his ears back.

"Stay safe, hide in the trees," Quinn said. "We don't want you to be caught again."

Quickthorn tossed his black mane and pawed the ground with one enormous hoof. His spiraling horn glinted, its point as sharp as a skewer.

"It's been a grand adventure," Tom said. "We couldn't have done it without you."

Sebastian contented himself with patting the unicorn's silvery-brown back so hard, clouds of dust rose up and stung his eyes. "Stupid dust," he choked, wiping his eyes with his sleeve.

"I'll come looking for you as soon as I can," Elanor promised. "I . . . I do hope you'll still be here."

Quickthorn harrumphed and nudged her with his nose. Elanor hugged him one more time, then left the unicorn and made her reluctant way down the path to the pebbly beach where the coracles had been left.

The others kept close, though nobody spoke.

Quickthorn whinnied and trotted after them. "No, boy. Stay here," Elanor said. "Please." He shook his horned head and came down the path behind them.

"You need to stay, Quickthorn. You can't come to the castle with us. There's water and grass here. You'll be safe." Elanor's voice was unsteady with tears.

The griffin soared away into the twilight sky and the dragon spread her wings and flew up to join him. Quickthorn's hooves crunched loudly on the pebbles as he reached the beach.

Sebastian pushed the coracles down to the water's edge. Quinn called to Sabre, who came slithering through the waves so that she could loop the ropes around his neck once more.

Tom jumped into his coracle, Wulfric tucked under his arm, and seized a paddle. Fergus leapt in, setting it rocking violently. Quinn and Elanor scrambled into their crafts. As Sebastian pushed the first coracle out into the waves, Quickthorn cantered down to the water's edge, neighing frantically. "Quick, Sebastian!" Tom called.

Sebastian heaved into his coracle, dripping wet, and Elanor pushed off the shore with the paddle. "I'm sorry, boy," she cried to Quickthorn. "You have to stay."

As the serpent began to swim strongly out to sea, the unicorn reared and neighed, then began to gallop along the beach, following them. "No, boy," Elanor wept. "Please! Stay!"

Quickthorn reached the rocky end of the beach, wheeled around and galloped back, pebbles spraying up from his hooves. He reached the place where the coracles had been launched and galloped into the water after them.

"Go back!" Elanor cried.

For a moment, it seemed as if the unicorn would swim after them, but as Quickthorn reached deeper water, he stopped, rearing up again and again, neighing, water frothing around his hocks. Then he turned and cantered back to the shore, mane and tail streaming. He disappeared from sight as the coracles were towed around the headland.

Elanor rubbed her eyes. "Will I ever see him again?"

"Of course you will," Sebastian answered stoutly, but he could not look at her.

4

THE
WARSHIP

Mist coiled around the coracles in clammy white tendrils. Quinn shivered at the touch on her face. She drew a torn piece of fabric up over her mouth, remembering all too well how the mist had numbed her mind and lulled her into an enchanted sleep the last time she had been here.

The sea serpent had brought the coracles right to the mouth of the harbor, where they bobbed up and down in the rough swell. "Thank you, Sabre," Quinn whispered. "We have to leave you here. I . . . I hope I see you again."

The sea serpent bowed his head and she reached to stroke his silky scales before untying the rope that attached the coracles to him. Then the sea serpent sank away beneath the waves, a flick of his long tail sending spray high into the air.

The children paddled their basket boats through the narrow gap between the headland and the stone causeway. For a few minutes, the coracles were tossed up and down like corks in a storm drain, but then they shot through into the calmer waters of the harbor. Keeping the motion of their paddles gentle to avoid the sound of splashing, they floated towards the town they knew was ahead, clustered at the base of the hill. The mist made it hard to see more than a few paces ahead. All was dark and quiet.

A huge dark shape loomed ahead of them. Before Quinn could dig in her paddle and stop her coracle, it thumped against the side. It was a huge ship, bigger than any Quinn had ever seen. It towered above them, a few lights piercing the gloom.

"It must be that warship Lord Mortlake was building," Tom whispered.

"It's incredible how fast they built it!" Sebastian said. "It looks ready to sail!"

To sail against the King, Quinn thought. *My great-uncle, Ivor.*

The thought made her edgy and afraid. Quinn didn't like to think about what could be the consequences of her discovery on the Lost Isles. On one hand, it was shiveringly exciting to know that she had royal blood. On the other hand, it was awful to know that both her parents were dead, and that her only living relative was a king most people thought of as frightening and cruel.

And what of her ambitions to be a Grand Teller? If it was true she was really some kind of princess, would they make her give up her study of magic? Would she have to wear shoes and mind her manners? Would they make her go and live at Stormholt Castle with her great-uncle? Quinn didn't want to. She wanted to stay here at Wolfhaven Castle with her friends.

"We'll have to go around it," Elanor whispered and began to paddle sideways.

Quinn began to paddle again, too. The warship was like a floating castle, its sides as steep as an overhanging cliff. They reached its stern and began to edge around it, sliding under the weed-hung anchor chain. It was so thick, Quinn could not have wrapped the fingers of both hands around it and she wondered how huge the anchor must be.

She heard a faint squeaking sound and all the hairs on her neck rose. A huge black rat was perched on the anchor rope, peering down at her with gleaming red eyes. "Urrgh," she said and shrank back.

The squeaking intensified. Quinn saw more rats running down the chain towards her. They were all as large as hares. "Quick, let's get away!"

She tried to push away from the ship with her paddle. The first rat gave a high-pitched squeal and leapt for the coracle. Quinn batted it away with her paddle. More rats leapt at them from the ship, or raced down the anchor chain, squealing loudly. The rat that had landed in the water swam for Quinn's coracle and tried to scramble on board. She cried out in horror and whacked it hard with her paddle.

The noise rang out over the still water, and somewhere nearby a man shouted out. "Beware! Beware! Attackers!"

Lights kindled on the ship and on the shore. Men leaned over the ship's rail, holding lanterns high. Desperately, the children tried to paddle away into the mist-wreathed darkness, but giant rats swarmed all over their wicker boats. One latched on to Sebastian's boot and he kicked it away into the water. Quinn swept around her with her paddle, but there were so many. Too many.

Then two red lances of light shot down from the castle. They burned through the mist, parting the veils to show two women standing in the window of the highest tower. Lady Mortlake and Mistress Mauldred. The red light shone from the rings on their fingers.

Quinn's mouth dried. Her hands trembled in fear. Now the witch sisters knew they were here.

"So much for stealth," Sebastian muttered.

"They'll be hunting us now," Quinn said. "Let's get into the underground caves as fast as we can. They won't be able to see us then."

The children paddled as fast as they could away from the warship. The soldiers shot flaming arrows after them. One fell in Tom's coracle, but he quickly stamped it out. The harbor was alive with light now, every lantern kindled. Soldiers ran from every direction, many piling into rowing boats. The children had no hope of out-paddling them.

Quinn put two fingers into her mouth and whistled with all her strength. The shrill, high-pitched noise rang out. "Sabre!" she screamed. "I need you!"

A white arrow-shaped swell of water surged towards them. The sea serpent's great head reared from the water. With a glad leap of her heart, Quinn realized that the sea serpent must have been lurking nearby, standing guard over her.

"Sabre! Destroy the boat!" Quinn shouted, pointing at the immense warship.

The sea serpent dipped his head to her, then rose higher. There was a cry from the ship's watchman. As Sabre began to coil his great body around the ship, soldiers attacked it with their swords and shot flaming arrows at his head. All bounced off the sea serpent's armor-like scales.

"Good thinking!" Tom called, as he fitted an arrow to the string of his bow. "At the very least, we'll scupper Lord Mortlake's treasured boat!"

Beltaine was darting through the air, catching giant rats and swallowing them in a single gulp. Already her belly was distended. Still more rats swam towards the coracles, their eyes gleaming in the flaring light from the ship. The four friends paddled furiously to the causeway as Sabre twisted behind them, the ship creaking and cracking between his coils.

"No!" Lady Mortlake's shriek of rage echoed around the harbor. A red beam of light lashed out like a whip against Sabre, who hissed and released the ship. Timber shuddered as he sank beneath the waves.

"Sabre!" Quinn searched the tossing waters of the harbor desperately, praying that the serpent had not been harmed. "*Sabre!*"

"Quinn, come on!" Tom called.

A long groan from above. The mainmast of the ship was slowly toppling.

"It's coming straight for us!" Sebastian gasped. "Quick!" He seized his oar with renewed energy, paddling madly.

"We'll never get away in time!" Elanor cried,

covering her head with her arms.

With a hideous crack, the mast plummeted towards them.

In a welter of foam, Sabre reared from the water, his long sinuous body arching high above the coracles. The mast smashed down upon his coils. The sea serpent shrieked in pain, as the mast broke in two and disappeared into the water. With a last great effort, the sea serpent flicked his tail. The four boats were flung high into the air. Elanor screamed in terror. The little round boats whirled through the air, then landed, spinning, on the stone causeway. The children lay gasping as the last pieces of the warship's mast hit the water where they had been moments before, sending up great gouts of spray.

"Sabre! You saved us!" Quinn exclaimed, scrambling to her feet. The serpent bowed his head to her. Dark blood stained his scales.

"I take it all back," Tom gasped. "He *is* my friend. Right now, he's my best friend."

"Thank you!" Elanor said. Sebastian nodded, trying to catch his breath.

Red rays of light pierced the mist once more, stabbing, searching.

Quinn risked a look up at the tower. Mistress Mauldred and Lady Mortlake stood side by side, their arms flung high. The light blazing from their rings filled the night with a ghastly reddish glow. Behind them crouched an old hunchbacked woman, leaning on a staff. It was Wilda, the witch of the Witchwood. *The giant rats would be her doing*, Quinn thought.

"Rex!" Tom shouted. "Come to me."

The flapping of great wings sent the mist swirling away as the griffin swooped down out of the darkness. Tom leapt onto his back.

"What are you doing?" Quinn shouted.

Tom pointed up at the tower. "I'm going to stop those witches!"

"No! It's too dangerous!" Quinn called back.

But the griffin was already soaring towards the tower, Tom crouched on his back and fitting an arrow to his bow.

5

THE
IRON CAGE

Tom gripped his knees tightly into Rex's feathers. Flaming arrows zinged towards them, but the griffin swerved around them.

"To the tower!" Tom cried. Rex soared into the sky.

The red light hurt Tom's eyes. He averted his gaze and saw—hanging on the side of the tower—a cage made of iron. Someone was crouched within.

Tom had no time to do more than glance. Giant ravens swooped out from the tower, claws raking. Rex dived away, then spun and shot up past them. The ravens attacked from all directions as the griffin fought back. Ravens shrieked. Black feathers spun in the wind.

Talons tore at Tom's shirt and he cried out in pain as they wrenched him sideways. Helpless, Tom slid off Rex's back. He dropped his bow, reaching desperately for something to grab.

There was nothing but air.

Tom tumbled down, down, down.

Red rays of light pierced the mist, stabbing, searching.

"We need to get under cover," Elanor cried. "They know we're here, they're looking for us."

And then they heard it, muffled and faint, as though from far away.

Slap, slap, slap.

Snuff, snuff, snuff.

The bog-men were coming.

Through the dizzy reel of red-hued darkness, Tom saw the iron cage spinning towards him. He reached out desperately. One hand managed to catch at the bars. Just as his fingers slipped free, he caught another bar with his other hand. The cage swung wildly. Tom risked a glance down. Darkness yawned below him. The warship was as small as a bath toy, and the flaming arrows shooting from all directions were as tiny as sparks from a campfire.

He must not fall.

Sebastian caught Elanor's hand. "Run!"

She gathered up her wet, ragged skirts and bolted along the causeway. Fergus snarled as bog-men loped out of the darkness. He and the wolf cub leapt for two of the bog-men's throats, bearing them down to the ground. Quinn vaulted over the fallen bog-men, running as fast as she could. Behind her, the sea serpent hissed in pain as an arrow pierced the torn skin of its back. Quinn faltered and looked back. "Go, Sabre!" she screamed. "Get out of here."

The sea serpent thrashed from side to side as more arrows pierced its flesh. Then it sank away under the black waters, froth churning up around as it disappeared.

"Sabre!"

As Quinn shouted, she was suddenly seized from behind by two skinny, leathery arms. She smelled the stink of the swamp. Desperate, she fought to break free, but the strength of the bog-man's arms was astonishing. Slowly, she was forced down to her knees, the sharp point of its spear at her throat.

"Grab my hand!" a voice cried.

Looking up, Tom saw a dirty white face peering at him through the bars of the cage. A small hand reached down for him. With a great effort, Tom managed to catch hold of the outstretched hand. *He'll never be strong enough to drag me up*, he thought grimly. But the hand gripped his with surprising strength.

Tom was dragged up and managed to get one foot in through the bars of the cage. A raven swooped at him, but he managed to swing away. Tom looked at the boy in the cage for the first time. He saw a filthy ragged creature with tangled dark curls and bright black eyes and a wicked-looking grin that Tom knew all too well.

It wasn't a boy at all.

"Jack!" Tom cried. "What are you doing here?"

"I guess you didn't come all this way to rescue me."

"Well, no . . . we thought you were miles away! What happened?"

"I was caught trying to get to Sebastian's father. They dragged me back here. Lady Mortlake was not pleased to see me. They locked me in this cage and lowered me over the edge of the tower. I think she hoped you'd come back to try and rescue me, then get caught in her trap."

Tom had first met Jack when she'd jumped out of a pie at the midsummer feast more than a month ago.

Lord Mortlake had gifted Jack to Elanor to act as her fool, to amuse and run errands for her, but in reality Jack had been the Mortlakes' spy, sent to help them invade Wolfhaven Castle. But Jack had not wanted to help her cruel masters, so she had slipped away during the invasion, taking Wolfhaven's silver with her. Later, she'd helped the children defeat the Beast of Blackmoor Bog and escaped with them. It was then they had learned that Jack was not a boy, but a girl in disguise.

She'd left them to take the news of the invasion to Sebastian's father, Lord Byrne of Ashbyrne Castle . . . but obviously had never made it.

The giant ravens were all around the cage now, wings flapping, beaks snapping. Tom's arms and legs were bruised and torn.

"I guess I'd better rescue you then," Tom said. "Can you get out of the cage?"

"That's not the problem," Jack replied, and wriggled her thin body through the bars of the cage. "There's no cage that can hold me. I'd have escaped ages ago if I could work out some way to get down to the ground without killing myself!"

"Rex!" Tom called.

The griffin swooped down on the cage, his talons sending one of the ravens tumbling away. Tom leapt onto his back and in an instant Jack was behind him, gripping him tightly around the waist. "Let's go!" she shouted and Rex soared away.

"Stop them! Kill them!" Mistress Mauldred screamed from the tower. A murder of ravens swept upon them. Tom could see nothing but black feathers and hear nothing but raucous shrieks.

Elanor spun on her heel. She saw Quinn in the grip of a bog-man. Bending, she picked up one of the heavy boulders from the side of the causeway and flung it with all her strength. The rock hit the bog-man in the side of the head, knocking him down. Quinn scrambled to her feet and raced to join her friends.

With the wolfhound and wolf cub leaping ahead of

them, and Beltaine swooping above their heads, they reached the safety of the narrow streets of the town. For a moment, Elanor thought they could escape into the misty darkness. But then a ray of red stabbed at them from the tower height. They were lit up in a circle of malevolent light.

The rats raced towards them, shrieking.

Tat-tat-tat! Tat-tat-tat!

The bog-men struck their spears so hard against the ground a little thunder rose into the sky. Looking up, Elanor saw hundreds of bog-men swarming down the rocky cliffs from the castle. They scuttled as swiftly as spiders.

Tat-tat-tat! Tat-tat-tat!

The mist swirled, showing just snatches of the bog-men's stick-thin leathery limbs, their bony eye sockets, their flared black nostrils. Closer and closer they came.

Elanor felt faint and dizzy. Quinn caught her by the arm. "Cover your mouth," she hissed. "Try not to breathe in the mist."

Obediently, Elanor folded a corner of her wet

ragged dress over her mouth and stumbled on. Rats swarmed up out of the dark waters of the harbor, filling the night with their hideous squeaks. Bog-men slithered down the walls and bounded out of every courtyard and alley, long spears held high. *Slap, slap, slap . . .*

Far above, ravens wheeled and squawked.

Then Elanor heard a high cry of pain.

Jack screamed as a raven stabbed her upper arm with its sharp beak.

"Hold on!" Tom shouted. He wheeled the griffin around. The great beast swooped and swerved and fought his way free. Higher and higher they soared, till the red searchlights of the witches' rings were lost far below them. The ravens fell away as the griffin burst through the red-hued mist. Above, an arching dome of radiant stars; below, a white landscape of soft, billowing clouds.

Tom's arms and legs were trembling, and he gripped as tightly as he could to Rex's feathery neck. He never wanted to fall again.

He heard Jack sniffle.

"Is all well?" he asked.

"More than well," Jack answered, wiping her nose on her tattered sleeve. "It's just . . . Oh, Tom, I always try to be brave, but I was so afraid you wouldn't come!"

"I'm sorry, we didn't know you'd been captured." He added, with as much nonchalance as he could muster, "So I guess this means Sebastian's father and his army are not riding to help us?"

"No," Jack said. "I'm so sorry. I tried to get away, but there were too many soldiers."

Tom's thoughts were racing. "I have to go back," he said.

"But . . . no!"

"I need to be with the others—we need to awaken the sleeping heroes. Do you think you could fly with Rex to find Sebastian's father, and get him here as fast as you can? It's several days' march . . . but you'll get to him tonight if you fly the whole way."

"Would—would the griffin let me fly on his back?" she asked hesitantly, not at all her usual cocky self. "Without you?"

"If you ask him nicely," Tom replied with a grin. The griffin shrieked and bucked, so that Jack screamed and wrapped her arms tighter around Tom's waist.

Tom sobered. "Don't be afraid. I think Rex understands how important it is. I will play to him and try and make him understand."

He fumbled in his pocket and found his flute. Then, gripping tightly with his knees so he would not fall, he lifted the flute to his mouth and began to play. He tried to pour all of his hopes and fears into the tune he played—his longing to see his mother again and his fear that she may have been hurt; his anger at the cruel way Lord Mortlake and the witches had imprisoned all the castle folk; his desperate hope that he and his friends may succeed in their impossible quest and raise the sleeping heroes of legend. The music rose high into the starry sky, wild and sweet, and the griffin glided, his head turned so he could fix Tom with one hooded golden eye.

At last, Tom could play no longer, the lump in his throat making it hard to breathe. He quickly dragged his sleeve across his eyes.

Jack whispered, "That was beautiful."

"Will you fly Jack to safety, Rex?" Tom asked. "Then come back and find me, and help me?"

The griffin inclined his majestic feathered head.

"Then you need to take me back down." As he spoke, Tom tucked away his flute, marveling once again at the way music calmed the great beast.

The griffin wheeled and flew back down. Within seconds, the beast and his double burden were muffled in cloud and mist again. Then they swooped below the cloud cover.

And plunged into screaming chaos.

ON THE BRIDGE

Elanor ran through the fog-bound streets, her breath sharp in her chest.

The red rays of light from the tower swept the streets, searching for them. She and her friends did their best to stay in the shadows, but behind them came the *slap, slap, slap* of leathery feet hitting stone and the *snuff, snuff, snuff* of nostrils flaring at their scent. They had to make it to the bridge and the secret entrance to the caves, else all was lost.

Tears blinded Elanor. She tripped and sprawled, grazing the palms of her hands and bruising her knees. Sebastian helped her up. He murmured words of encouragement, even while fending off the rats that now leapt on either side of them. Sword-less, he punched one away and kicked another. "Get off, you filthy beasts," he shouted. "Leave Ela be!"

They staggered on, Beltaine flaming at the rats.

The bridge loomed ahead of them, a dark humpbacked shape rising out of mist. They heard the swishing of giant wings. With amazement, Elanor recognized Jack clinging behind Tom. He leapt down, and Jack and the griffin soared away into the darkness.

"Where have you been?" Quinn panted.

"Tell you later. Run!"

They ran to the bridge. Armored knights ran to meet them, swords flashing. Elanor fought desperately, but it was no good. The knights were too big, too strong, too well armed. One knocked her dagger out of her hands and seized her. "Won't my lord be pleased with me? I have the little lady!"

Elanor struggled with all her strength. The knight had his arm tight around her waist, the chain mail cutting her cruelly. Sebastian fought to get to her, but was tackled to the ground by two knights in heavy black armor.

Another seized Tom from behind, then swung his sword at Fergus. "Down, boy!" Tom shouted.

The wolfhound obediently dropped to his haunches, and the sword swung harmlessly over his head. "Stay!" Tom shouted, then yelled at the knight, "Don't kill him! He'll stay, he'll stay."

The knight menaced the big dog with the point of his sword, but Fergus stayed down, every muscle tense and ready to spring.

They were surrounded on all sides. Knights in gleaming black armor. Rats with beady red eyes. Hundreds of bog-men creeping out of a swirl of foul-smelling fog. Far above, the searching lances of red light from the witch sisters' rings pierced the gloom and once again found and pinned them.

Elanor felt sick. She feared her old governess Mistress Mauldred even more than she feared the bog-men. The very thought of being caught and taken back to her made Elanor's knees weaken.

Quinn caught her arm. "Stand tall," she whispered. "Don't let them know how afraid we are."

"We need to get to the underground caves," Tom

whispered. "If we could just jump off the bridge, we could swim to the secret door in seconds."

A tall figure in black armor loomed out of the mist, parting the bog-men like a wave. His face was covered with a visor, but Elanor recognized him at once by the boar tusks that crowned his helmet.

Lord Mortlake laughed in triumph, the sound booming through the iron of his visor. "Caught at last!" he gloated. "What trouble you've caused me! Foul little pests, I should've squashed you long ago."

Beltaine swooped from the darkness, hissing and spitting sparks.

"No!" Sebastian cried. But it was too late. Lord Mortlake seized the little dragon from the air in one huge iron gauntlet.

"Well, *this* looks useful," he drawled. Beltaine spat again. "Ah, but you need to learn some manners, don't you?" He clamped one fist tightly around the dragon's muzzle. Though the dragon struggled and scratched, she made no impression on his heavy black armor.

Elanor felt dread roiling in the pit of her stomach, but tried to square her shoulders and lift her chin.

Lord Mortlake made a slashing gesture with one hand. "Kill them!"

The knights lifted their swords, keen edges catching the red light so it seemed as if the blades shone with blood.

At that moment, a neigh rent the night. A huge dark shape came galloping over the bridge, hooves thundering on the cobblestones. Elanor saw the glint of a long spiraling horn. "Quickthorn!" she cried.

The unicorn reared over her, wielding his horn with wicked intent. The knight who held Elanor so tightly was knocked down. Elanor found herself suddenly and unexpectedly free.

"Thank you, Quickthorn!" she cried.

The unicorn attacked the knights holding the others. In moments, they too were free.

"Jump!" Tom cried.

He lifted Elanor up to the stone parapet. She looked back. The unicorn was surrounded on all sides by knights, swords flashing. Quinn was already up on the stone parapet. "Come on!" she cried and jumped into the darkness.

"Quickthorn," Elanor sobbed.

Sebastian was looking back as well. "Beltaine!" he called. The little dragon struggled desperately to be free, but she was held firm by hard hands.

"We have to go," Tom said. "I'm sorry!"

He pushed Elanor off the parapet.

Elanor fell, arms flailing. She landed with a great splash in the cold, dark river. Seconds later, Sebastian and Tom jumped into the water beside her. Then, whining, the wolfhound leapt from the parapet.

They swam forward, Tom carrying the squirming wolf cub in his arms.

Quinn found the handle and the hidden door swung up. The four children swam inside, Fergus paddling behind, and the door swung shut behind them. All was pitch-black.

Elanor's questing foot felt something beneath her, slimy and icy cold. "There's ground here," she said, and heard the others splashing towards her.

"They'll be after us in a moment," Tom said. "Is there any way to lock the door behind us?"

"I don't know," Quinn said. "It's too dark."

"If Beltaine was here, she could spit out flames for us to see by," Sebastian said. "You should have let me rescue her, Tom."

"There were too many of them, Sebastian," Tom said. "We had to get away."

Elanor could not speak. Her mind's eye filled with images of the unicorn fighting. "Quickthorn saved us," she managed to whisper at last. "We can't let his sacrifice be in vain."

"They won't kill him," Quinn said, her voice quivering. "Lord Mortlake wants him."

"Lord Mortlake wants his *horn*," Elanor corrected her. "He does not know he only has to wait till winter and Quickthorn will shed it. Lord Mortlake will kill him for it."

Tears overflowed. She wiped them away from her frozen cheeks. Her ring grazed her cheek and she remembered the Traveler's Stone. It took her a moment to catch her breath so she could blow on it. A silvery-blue light flickered up.

She and her friends were standing chest deep in rippling green water. Heavy white stalactites hung above their heads. The stone ceiling curved down on either side, enclosing them within a small cavern. To their left, the cavern receded into shadows, but Elanor could see the faint glimmer of light on water.

"That's the way we need to go," Quinn said. "Remember, we sailed down a narrow river to this cavern and I opened the gate with that hanging chain." She pointed at a chain that hung down near the hidden gate behind them.

At that very moment, they heard banging outside.

"We have to secure that door!" Sebastian cried.

Quinn dived into the water and swam across to the water gate. She searched hurriedly and found heavy wooden bolts that slammed into place. She swam swiftly back to her friends, her face drained of all color. "It won't take them long to break through. The bolts are only made of wood."

"Let's go!" Tom cried.

Dripping wet, shivering with cold, the four children scrambled up the rocky slope and raced alongside the underground river. Fergus trotted ahead of them, his eyes gleaming in the light of the Traveler's Stone whenever he turned his head to look back at them. Wulfric kept close to Tom's heels, not liking this cold, dark, echoing place.

After a while, they came to a wide lake, its waters gleaming a strange translucent green under the silver radiance of Elanor's ring. When they had last been here, they had found Arwen's boat, Owl-Eyes. Now the lake was empty. Elanor felt a pang of sadness, remembering the boat being swallowed by the sea monster's maw.

"I'm so cold," she said, hugging herself. Her wet clothes dragged on her and she was trembling with exhaustion. Her arm ached from holding it high so the ring lit their way.

"There's a lantern," Quinn said, pointing ahead. "Let's see if we can light it."

"All our tinder will be wet," Sebastian said. "If Beltaine were here, she could light it."

"Shut up!" Elanor finally shouted. "We know you're upset, Sebastian! We've all lost our beasts, too."

There was a stunned silence. It was so unlike Elanor to speak in such a way.

Sebastian turned red. After a moment, he muttered, "Sorry."

"No, I'm sorry," Elanor said. "I shouldn't have yelled." For an instant, she heard an echo of Mistress Mauldred's voice, nagging at her: *Ladies must never raise their voices.* She swallowed hard. "I'm so afraid for Quickthorn . . . and for my father . . ."

And for us too, she thought to herself, as the light from her ring began fading away.

"We'll just have to do our best to get a spark going," Quinn said. "Sebastian, do you have the tinderbox?"

He fumbled around in his pack. In a few moments, they heard the familiar sound of steel scraping on flint. The lantern warmed into life.

Just then, they heard a distant crash.

"The water gate!" Quinn cried. "They've broken through!"

7

I SLEEP BY DAY, I FLY BY NIGHT

The pound of running feet echoed through the dark caverns.

Quinn ran till she thought her heart would burst. Sebastian slipped and fell over. Elanor dragged him up. They kept on running.

"Where will the sleeping heroes be?" Tom panted.

"I . . . I don't know," Quinn admitted. "Arwen said under the castle."

"We shall have to explore every passage and every cavern," Sebastian said. "With soldiers on our trail."

"And bog-men," Elanor panted. "I can smell them."

"They're getting closer!" Quinn ran faster.

Through the narrow, twisting passageways the four

friends ran, climbing over rock falls, squeezing under stalactites, slipping on the damp white stone and clambering up again.

The soldiers almost caught them. Sebastian heaved up a great boulder and threw it. *Clang!* One of the soldiers fell in a heap. The men following him tripped over his prone figure and came crashing down. The children raced free.

Quinn recognized the occasional landmark—a rock shaped like a throne, a pool of water that gleamed emerald green in the swinging light of their lantern, a passageway that led only to a small cell where manacles still hung from the wall.

And always from behind them, the sound of bog-men, snuffling, searching.

Tom led them down a passageway they had never explored before. It opened up into a vast cavern, like a giant's great hall. Far above was a hole that led to the sky. Quinn could see stars out there.

The darkness above them was full of a constant soft susurration. *Whoosh, whoosh, whoosh . . .*

"What's that sound?" Elanor whispered.

Fergus growled up at the roof of the cavern. Wulfric barked, high and shrill, and the rustling grew in speed and volume.

"Something's up there." Quinn gazed upward.

She heard Sylvan's weary old voice in her mind. *I sleep by day, I fly by night. I have no feathers to aid my flight.* Quinn put up her hand to hold the wooden medallion that hung around her neck.

What is it? she asked.

I see without seeing, but I am not blind, it is with my voice that I seek and I find.

Elanor covered her nose. "It smells awful."

Fergus whined, looking up into the darkness above. The hair bristled along his spine.

"Listen! They're coming," Quinn whispered.

Slap, slap, slap.

Snuff, snuff, snuff.

"Quick! Hide!" Elanor saw a dark space behind a barrier of stalagmites and squeezed in. The others followed hurriedly. Sebastian shuttered their lantern and darkness fell upon them like a heavy cloak. Tom kept his hand clamped firmly over Wulfric's muzzle and Elanor crouched down, both arms around Fergus's hairy neck. Quinn hoped that the strong odor of the cave would hide their scent from the bog-men's sniffing nostrils.

"What's that horrible smell?" one knight said.

"It's your armpits," another replied.

"More like your feet!" the first knight cried, and got a shove in return that sent his armor clanking.

Sniff, sniff, snuffled the bog-men.

Whoosh, whoosh, whispered the darkness.

"What's that sound?" another knight said.

"That's your knees knocking together, you coward," another jeered.

"No, it's his teeth chattering!" a third cried.

"It's those rotten bog-men sniffing away. They give me the creeps," another said.

"This place gives me the creeps."

"You give me the creeps."

Meanwhile, the rustling grew and grew. Quinn craned her neck to see past Sebastian's shoulder.

"What's that moving?" One knight stared up into the darkness. "There's something up there."

Tiny winged shapes were fluttering around in an agitated cloud. Some darted past the hole to the outside world and Quinn saw the serrated edge of their wings.

Bats! The cave was full of bats.

An idea came to her. She grasped her witch's staff with both hands and bent her head. "*Grow, little bats, grow. Grow and fly low. Shriek, little bats, shriek. Shriek through the dark and bleak.*" She raised her staff and banged as hard as she could against the rock.

Tom gasped and gripped her tight, shushing her, but Quinn could feel the waves of magical energy rolling out. "Cover your ears!" she hissed to her friends.

The bats began to screech. The sound echoed around the cavern, hitting their ears like bullets. The bats' wings rustled madly. Quinn strained her eyes to see in the darkness. She was sure the bats were growing bigger and bigger and bigger. One swooped past the starry opening. It was huge!

Giant bats swooped around the knights and the bog-men. The knights tried to fight them off with their swords, but the bats were quick and nimble. One knight dropped his lantern and it rolled away, illuminating the scene in macabre flashes of light.

"Let's get out of here before they suck our blood!" one screamed. The knights stampeded out of the cave.

The bats were in a panic, swooping around and shrieking loudly. Then they found the starlit hole that led to the world outside. The hole soon thronged with giant wings as the bats flew out into the night. Gradually the sound of their shrieking died away, and the cave fell silent again.

"Are they all gone?" Elanor whispered.

"I think so," Quinn replied, smiling. She was shaken, but also exultant. She had wrought another spell of true power. "Those idiots! Bats eat insects. They don't drink human blood."

"They'll be out there in the night now, searching for something to eat." Tom un-shuttered the lantern, so a thin ray of light pierced the darkness. "Let's hope one of them mistakes Lord Mortlake for a giant bug."

They crawled out from the crevice. Suddenly Fergus raised one paw. He growled deep in his throat, his eyes gleaming in the scant light from the lantern.

Sniff, sniff, sniff . . .

All the hairs rose on Quinn's arms. She peered into the shadows. Hunched in the darkness, their nostrils flaring, were dozens of bog-men. They were smelling here and there, their acute sense of smell blunted by the stench of bat droppings.

Quinn gestured urgently to the others. Sebastian opened his mouth to speak, but she shushed him, pointing into the shadows. When he saw the bog-men crouched there, feeling the floor with their leathery fingers, sniffing at what they found, his tawny eyes dilated. Quinn put her finger to her lips, then pointed towards the dark tunnel that led away from the cave.

Step by slow step, the four friends tiptoed past the bog-men. Tom had the wolf cub in his arms, one hand around his muzzle. Quinn rested her hand on Fergus's ruff. She could hear the slow drip, drip, drip of water and the constant snuffling of the bog-men.

They were awful-looking creatures, their skin like ancient leather wrapped around bones. Each rib and the knobbly joints of knees and elbows were outlined.

Their eye sockets were hollow, their stomachs pressed flat to their spines. Long ago, their bodies had been thrown into the swamps, only to be raised to unnatural life hundreds of years later with the magic of a dragon's tooth. They could not see, but they could hear and they could smell.

It was hard to creep past them. Quinn hardly dared breathe.

Squeak, squeak—

The shrill noise broke the heavy silence. Quinn spun around, her pulse thumping in her ears. A giant rat was raised up on its hind legs, staring at her with red beady eyes. *Squeak, squeak.*

Another rat scuttled near, whiskers twitching. Then Quinn saw, to her horror, a whole river of rats racing towards her, sounding the alarm.

The bog-men lurched into action, reaching out to grab at the children.

Quinn and her friends could do nothing but try to outrun them.

APPLE REVERSED

The four friends raced through dark vast caverns and narrow twisting passageways, climbing over mounds of fallen stone and crawling under needles of white dripping stone.

The bog-men were so close behind, Quinn could smell their foul breath. The wolfhound did his best to guard the children, dragging down one bony, leathery creature after another. Wulfric nipped at the bog-men's ankles or tripped them over, and snapped at the rats whose shrill cries echoed around the caverns, guiding the blind bog-men forward.

"Look! There's a crevice ahead. It looks like it could lead somewhere," Sebastian called. "Quinn, see if you can wriggle through. I'll keep off the rats."

She squeezed herself into the narrow crack in the wall. "It does lead somewhere!" she called back. "I can feel air on my cheek."

She scrambled through, dragging the sea serpent scale behind her. Elanor followed easily, being the smallest, but Tom had more trouble. At last he scraped through, pulling the reluctant wolf cub behind him by the scruff of his neck. The lean wolfhound bounded after them, leaving Sebastian alone, facing an advancing circle of bog-men, spears raised high. They closed in, their tall spindly shadows creeping over the walls towards him. Rats thronged at their feet, eyes glowing red in the light of the lantern, whiskers twitching, tails whipping.

Sebastian had broken off two sharp stalactites and was keeping the creatures at bay with them. Now he flung them with all his strength at the rats. As they raced away, they tripped over the bog-men behind them, giving Sebastian a few seconds to get through the crevice. He scraped his shoulders painfully on the walls.

As he crept out the far side, he kicked hard at the

stalactites hanging from the roof of the passageway. He rolled free just in time as they crashed down. A great cloud of white dust rose. When it cleared, they saw that the narrow tunnel was blocked with rocks.

"Are you all right?" Elanor cried.

Sebastian jumped up, brushing off the dust. "Of course! That's stopped them for a little while at least. Let's go."

They stumbled on, guarding the frail light of their lantern. Once, as they stepped over a shallow puddle that filled the passageway, Quinn saw a glint of red light from within it. She told herself it was just the reflection from the lanterns, but it took a while for her heartbeat to slow again.

They could not find any sign of the sleeping heroes of the prophecy. The vast underground caverns and tunnels were empty.

"I don't think I can stand this much longer," Sebastian said, after a very long while.

"The lantern is guttering," Tom said. "Soon we'll be in complete darkness. Then what shall we do?"

"We'll have the Traveler's Stone," said Elanor,

though she was so weary that its light would only be frail. Then an idea struck her. "Why don't I try asking it to guide us to the sleeping heroes?"

The others crowded around her in excitement as she breathed on her ring then asked, "Where do the sleeping heroes lie?"

A dim ray of blue light rose from the ring, pointing upward to a ceiling hung with sharp needles of stone. Some reached down to touch tall pillars that rose from the cavern floor, others created lacy falls and fans of stone, like intricate candelabras.

Tom climbed the side of a thick pillar and peered into the darkness. "There's no hole or cave up here," he said. The others searched too, climbing all over the cave. There was no way up.

"Which way do we go?" Elanor asked the ring again. "Show us the way."

But the light only shone up. "*Up?* But there is no way up!" Elanor slumped in disappointment.

"Perhaps we need to find another way," Quinn said.

On they walked, exploring every fissure and

crevice. The lantern guttered out. They had to stumble on with no other light than the faint gleam of Elanor's moonstone ring, which sank lower and lower. Soon they were stumbling along in virtual darkness and the ring did not brighten, no matter how much Elanor breathed on it.

"We've searched every passageway in this place," Sebastian said. "The sleeping heroes are not here."

Tears sprung into Quinn's eyes. She had been thinking the same thought for the last two hours, but could not bear to say it out loud.

Elanor gazed out into the close-pressing darkness. "We're running out of time. We are meant to wake the sleeping heroes by dawn."

"I feel like we've been stuck down here for days," Tom said.

"What if it was just a story after all?" Sebastian's voice was bitter with disappointment.

"No!" Quinn clasped her hands together. "Arwen always speaks true. The sleeping heroes are here somewhere. They must be!"

"They aren't, Quinn. You're just going to have to

admit it. Your precious Arwen was spinning us a bag of moonshine." Sebastian sat down and bent his head into his hands. Tom dropped beside him, putting one hand on his friend's shoulder.

Quinn said nothing. Her feet hurt, her legs hurt, her heart hurt.

Do not lose faith, little maid, Sylvan said in her mind. *Remember the words of the story, remember the words of the spell.*

Quinn tried. She was too tired.

In the heart of every acorn is a forest, in the heart of every apple seed is an orchard. What is in thy heart, little maid? Darkness and despair? Or courage and cleverness? Dig deep, little maid, be brave and think. The Oak King's voice was gentle but firm. Elanor looked up.

"He's right," she said.

Quinn put her head in her hands. She was so cold in her damp clothes, she could not stop shivering and her stomach was hollow. She thought about what Sylvan had said. *Be brave and think . . .*

Quinn took a deep breath and raised her head.

"I'll read the tell-stones. Perhaps they can tell us

where to search." Quinn crouched down, drawing out a stone from the pouch and laying it on the ground before her. Elanor knelt down beside her, blowing on the ring. The light flickered and rose just enough for them all to see the rune painted on the pebble.

"The rune of the Ring. That means we have come to the end of something and the beginning of another."

"Perhaps it means we have reached the end of the caves and need to search elsewhere," Elanor said.

"But where?" Sebastian asked.

Quinn drew out another stone and laid it down. She felt a sickening lurch in the pit of her stomach.

"It's the Apple," Elanor said. She screwed up her face as she tried to remember. "Fruition? Success?"

"It's upside down," Quinn said faintly. "That means rot and failure."

There was a long silence.

Quinn laid down another stone. "Dark Moon. Darkness and black magic."

The light in the ring flickered.

Quinn drew out the last stone and laid it down, so that the four stones were set in a circle, one at each point of the compass. It was the sign of the Skull.

It meant Death.

Nobody spoke. Quinn gathered up the stones and dropped them back into her bag.

"What are we to do?" Elanor whispered.

"There's nothing we can do," Quinn said bleakly. "Unless you want to search the caverns again?"

"There's no point." Tom's head was bent, his hands hanging limply between his knees. Wulfric whined and laid his head on his lap.

"We've crawled through every crevice in every cave," Sebastian said. "It's useless."

"We need to rest," Elanor said. "We've been running and fighting for hours." She slid down so she was sitting on the ground. She rubbed her arms. "I'm so cold. So very cold."

Sebastian drew closer to her, putting his arm around her shoulders. Elanor leaned her head against his chest, trying to hide her tears.

Quinn let her head fall back. She stared up at the roof of the cavern, stalactites gleaming like daggers aimed for her heart. "We've failed."

No one spoke. Tom hid his face in his hands. Slowly the light ebbed out of the moonstone ring. Darkness choked them, as cold tendrils of mist wrapped around them.

There are no sleeping heroes.

It was only a story after all.

9

DREAMS

Sebastian dreamed that he was in an iron cage. It was so small that the bars pressed into his flesh and forced his head down between his knees. Ravens flapped all around the cage, pecking at him with their sharp beaks. He struggled to get away, but the cage was too small. The iron bars squeezed tighter and tighter. Sebastian exerted all his strength, trying to burst the cage open. It was too strong. He gripped the bars in both hands and shook them. He could not break free.

A tall figure loomed over him, dressed in black metal with boar tusks curving from his helmet. A cruel voice boomed out. "Look! If it's not Lord Byrne's half-wit son. Caught in my trap like the fool he is. What would your father think if he saw you now, boy? He'd be so disappointed . . . no wonder he sent you away! He knew you'd be a failure as a knight."

The words hurt Sebastian more than the stabbing beaks of the ravens. "That's not true!"

"You thought you could prevail against *me?*" Lord Mortlake sneered. "I shall carve you up into little pieces and send you back to your father. I shall send your father one of your ears and tell him he must face me in combat if he wishes to have the rest of you back. Then I shall hack *him* to pieces. Your castle, your lands, everything shall be mine!"

"No!" Sebastian struggled with all of his strength, but could not break free of the iron bars.

"You're a disappointment," Lord Mortlake jeered as he bent and seized Sebastian's ear between his metal-encased fingers. "And you'll be the cause of your father's death and your mother's despair."

Sebastian screamed as his ear was twisted from his head.

Quinn was caught in the midst of a thorny thicket, brambles snagging in her clothes, her hair, her skin. All around, thistles and stinging nettles entwined with deadly nightshade and wolfsbane. Ivy and bindweed wrapped around her wrists and throat.

An old hunchbacked woman stood before her, rats swarming around the tattered hem of her filthy skirts. Around her neck hung strings of wooden beads, seed pods, feathers and shells. A raven sat upon one shoulder, its beady eyes fixed on Quinn.

The old woman leaned on a twisted witch's staff. "You thought to be a witch?" Wilda taunted. "You thought to learn the mysteries of magic and gain yourself power? You're not even strong enough to stop us *watching* you. You thought you tricked us with that pathetic ruse? Children made from willow sticks? *Ha!* We knew it was a hoax. We wanted you to think you were safe so you would come back here, where we wanted you. There was never a moment when I did not have my eye upon you."

Quinn struggled to free herself, but the more she struggled, the tighter her bonds grew. She cried out in pain as the thorns dug into her flesh. Wilda stepped closer, grinning so widely Quinn could see how few teeth she had left in her rotting gums.

"And having failed at being a witch, you thought you'd make yourself queen? You'd believe any story if it made you feel that you're worth something. It's all lies, lies, lies!" Wilda hissed. "Your father was not a king and your mother certainly no queen. They abandoned you because they did not want you."

Quinn cried out, "No, that's not true! None of it's true! I've won my witch's staff . . . I've worked spells of power . . . and my father was the king!"

Wilda rocked with laughter. "You poor, deluded fool. Useless. Worthless. Unwanted. You're *nothing*." She raised her witch's staff and brought it down hard on Quinn's head, again and again. Quinn was knocked smaller with each blow. "You're nothing," the old witch said over and over as the blows fell.

The blows kept raining down on her head. With

each blow, Quinn shrank till she was no bigger than a pin head. One more blow and she would be a mere particle of dust. Another, and she'd be gone.

The witch's staff rose and fell, and rose once more.

Tom stood at a kitchen sink, scrubbing a pot. Dirty dishes towered high on either side of him, all caked with filth. As hard as he scrubbed, Tom could not clean away the food encrusted on the bottom. The water in the sink was as thick as soup with bits of old food. His hands were red and swollen.

"You're nothing but a pot boy," a voice whispered in his ear. He looked around, wiping sweat from his brow with one raggedy sleeve.

A black-haired woman reclined behind him on a high throne built of soup pots and dirty wooden spoons. She was wearing a gown of red silk embroidered with roses and lilies, and her skin was as fair and soft as the inside of a petal. Tom was embarrassed by his filthy rags, his sweat-damp hair.

"You dream of making your fortune," Lady Mortlake whispered. "You think you'll play a flute of gold and strum a harp inlaid with jewels. You imagine being the greatest minstrel the world has ever known. It's an impossible dream. A pot boy you were born and a pot boy you'll remain."

Tom's shoulders slumped. He looked down at the filthy sink water.

"All you're good at is scrubbing pots and peeling potatoes," Lady Mortlake told him. "All your friends will go on to the royal court. She'll be queen, and they'll be her knight and her maid-in-honor. And you'll be left here, cooking and cleaning, scrubbing and scouring—"

"Stop it!" Tom cried. "Please."

But her voice whispered on. "Washing and wiping, sweeping and swiping . . ."

Tom wiped his dripping hands over his face.

It was all true. He was nothing but a pot boy.

Elanor ran through the vast, shadowy castle. Her breath sobbed. A stitch stabbed her side. She could not stop, though. Someone was hunting her.

A red spotlight flashed on her. It shocked her with pain. "You can't hide from me," a woman's voice said, cold with hatred.

Elanor ran on, cold stone bruising her feet. She ran through empty halls and galleries, through rooms that lay abandoned under dustcovers. Behind her, the red light probed through the darkness. Every time it touched her heel or glanced across her cheek, it burned like a thousand wasp stings. Elanor could not help crying aloud in pain and terror.

"Father!" she called. "Help me! Where are you?"

Mocking laughter replied. "You think that pathetic old man can help you? He's hardly noticed you for years. He cared only for your mother. Once she died, he wanted to be dead too. He didn't care enough to want to live for your sake. I have watched it all. Well, he has had his wish. He's dead now, too. You're an orphan. And there's no one left to care what happens to you."

Elanor stumbled and fell. The red light skimmed across her back and she jerked away from the jolt of it. Like a fiery lance, the red light pinned her down.

"Did you really think you could hide from me?" Mistress Mauldred stood over Elanor. Her eyes were black holes. "I see you. I *know* you. And I shall kill you as you helped kill my mother."

She raised a fistful of red energy. Elanor screamed and scrambled to her feet to run again, through vast castle halls hung with cobwebs.

No matter how hard she ran, Mistress Mauldred was always striding close behind her, the red light from her ring stabbing at her. "Stop!" she commanded.

Elanor fell to her knees

"How dare you disobey me? Ladies must always obey their elders!" Mistress Mauldred began to strike her. Elanor struggled to rise, but her limbs were weighted with lead. As the witch's hand rose and fell, it made red streaks in the air as if it was made of flame.

Elanor flung up her hands to protect her face from the blows. "No!" she cried.

Suddenly blue light shone out from her moonstone ring. It radiated outward, like a shield of shimmering blue energy. The red light glanced off it. Mistress Mauldred cried out as if in pain.

The blue light grew stronger. It spun Elanor in a cocoon of electricity.

"Where are you? Show yourself to me!" Mistress Mauldred demanded.

Elanor peered through the blue haze of light. She could not see her governess any longer. The blue light wavered and thinned. She saw Mistress Mauldred's face bending towards her, her lips thin and cruel.

"Ladies must always do as they are told!"

"No," Elanor said.

The shield of blue light came up again, stronger than ever. Mistress Mauldred was knocked away. Shrieking, she disappeared. Elanor woke up, shivering and afraid, to find the moonstone ring was shining faintly in the darkness.

Somewhere above their heads, a cock crowed.

10

KEY OF BONE

"Wake up!"

Sebastian was jerked out of his nightmare by the sound of Elanor's voice. He groaned, cold and stiff from sleeping on the damp rocks of the underground cavern. The others all woke too, their faces white and strained.

Quinn's eyes were wild. "It's all lies! I'm a fool, to believe in such a bag of moonshine. I'm not a queen, and there are no heroes." She began to weep. "Wilda . . . she told me it was all a pack of lies."

Tom lay still on the damp stone, listening, his arm flung around the wolfhound's neck. His blue eyes were dulled by pain. "I . . . I had a nightmare too."

"Me too!" said Sebastian. "I dreamed I was in an iron cage, being pecked at by ravens."

"Like Jack!" Tom said. During the long hours they had wandered through the dark caves, he had told the others how he had rescued the imprisoned girl.

"The witches were trying to get to us in our sleep," Elanor said. "They want us to give up. In my dream, Mistress Mauldred caught me and told me I must be punished, that ladies must always do as they are told . . . but I managed to push her away with my ring."

Quinn scrubbed her wet face. "What are we to do now? It must be dawn by now, and we've found no trace of the mythical sleeping heroes. And they'll still be hunting us."

"Well, we have to go on, don't we?" Elanor said. "I mean, we've come so far . . . we can't give up now."

"But what's the use? There are no sleeping heroes." Quinn's voice was flat with misery.

"We don't have any weapons and all our beasts are gone or captured." Pain roughened Sebastian's voice at the memory of Beltaine trapped in Lord Mortlake's hands.

Elanor drew out the long, spiraling unicorn horn and hefted it in her hand. "We could try and use our beast's gifts as weapons."

Sebastian drew out the dragon tooth. "I guess I could make it into a dagger, it's sharp enough."

Quinn looked at the sea serpent scale, which lay on the ground nearby. She shrugged. "I could use it as a shield. I just need a handle of some kind." She looked around, then broke off a stalactite and wedged it into the back of the scale as a handle.

"What am I meant to do with the feathers?" Tom said miserably. "Tickle Lord Mortlake to death?" He hunched his shoulders. "How can we stand up against a whole army of bog-men?"

"There must be something we can do." Elanor looked around pleadingly.

"Sabre smashed up the warship in the harbor. That's something," Quinn said.

"What if we try and rescue all the prisoners from the dungeon?" Elanor suggested. "Sir Kevyn will be mad as a hornet over being locked up. Once free, he'll help us fight back."

"So would all the other knights and squires." Sebastian sat up. "If we raided the armory, we could take them all some weapons."

"We could ring the warning bell," Tom said. "We could ring it and let the townsfolk know that the castle has been seized. Then they would all help us!" His face suddenly lit up. "And my father will be nearby, in the forest. He said he'd come with his wolves when I needed him. If we rang the bell, he'd come!"

"We could rescue our beasts," Elanor said, her hazel eyes bright.

Sebastian jumped up with fresh energy. "I like the idea of us being the heroes! If only I had a sword! And my dragon! And an army of ten thousand!"

"At least we have each other," Elanor replied.

Tom got to his feet. "We'll have to be quick and quiet. They're searching the castle for us."

Sebastian lifted his dragon tooth high. "Arise, oh, sleeping heroes," he intoned. "It is time to go forth and make the lives of our oppressors a misery."

"We should open the war gate first, so that they can all get in to the castle," Tom suggested. "The key is in the Great Hall. That's just across the garden from here. Let's go and get that first."

"Yes, it makes sense to open up a line of retreat," Sebastian said. "Let's go!"

"We can sneak out the secret stairs that lead to Arwen's room in the old oak tree," Quinn said.

Elanor got to her feet, breathing once more on her ring till it glowed a little brighter. Holding it before her, she led the way through the caverns to the steps that led up to Arwen's home. They clambered up the secret stairs into the hollow trunk of the oak tree, then stood, looking around them sadly.

Arwen's room had always been bright and warm, with a fire glowing on the hearth and a cat curled up asleep on a cushion. Now all was desolate.

"Such a shame," Elanor said.

"We will save the castle so Arwen's tree can be a home once more," Quinn said.

Sebastian nodded, and Tom gave her a little pat of comfort. "Come on, let's go." He eased open the door and peeped outside, Fergus pushing his head against his hip in his eagerness to see, too.

The garden beyond the oak tree was still and quiet, shrouded in darkness. "We still have some time before dawn," Tom said. "That crowing cock must be befuddled by the mist. The darkness will help hide us."

Red spotlights probed the castle and inner ward, searching for them.

"Someone's going to have to deal with those witches," Sebastian said, peering over Tom's shoulder.

"I guess that has to be me," said Quinn.

"And me!" Elanor said quite unexpectedly. "After all, we think she may have killed my mother and cast an evil spell on my father! I want justice for that!"

The others all looked at her in amazement, remembering the timorous girl they had once known. She looked very different in her ragged dress, her hair in a mess, Quickthorn's horn in her hand.

"That's the spirit!" Sebastian said.

Together, the four friends crept across the lawn, Fergus and Wulfric at their heels. They paused under the shadow of an archway. A squad of guards marched past. They did not see the four children, crouched low in the darkness.

"The lord's in a rare taking," one said to another. "His ship's been crushed to tinder, I heard!"

"It's a bad sign," his friend whispered back. "Nothing they did could kill the sea beast!"

"Oh, thank goodness!" Quinn breathed.

Only then did Tom realize that her anxiety over Sabre's safety was as great as his fear for Rex.

The guards marched on. When they were long gone, the children crept out from under the hedge and ran for the great hall. As they reached the edge of the inner ward, a few birds began to chirrup. Looking up, Tom saw the hint of a silvery glow to the east. Dawn was perhaps half an hour away.

He led the way into the Great Hall. All the tables and benches had been pushed up against the wall. The rushes on the floor were old and smelled musty. At the far end of the room was a cold fireplace, big enough to roast an ox. Fergus and Wulfric bounded towards it. The mantelpiece above was ornately carved into leaf fronds and flower buds and the two prancing heraldic beasts of the Wolfhaven crest. Tom had almost forgotten the crest was there, so obscured it was by centuries of smoke. As they neared the fireplace, his eyes moved from Fergus and Wulfric to the carved stone beasts above them with a shiver of awe. A wolf and a wolfhound stood rampant. Their front paws lifted towards the two gigantic keys that were hung above, one crossed over the other. One of the keys was black and the other was ivory.

"The black key is cast from iron," Elanor whispered, "and the white key is carved from bone."

"Which one opens the gate?" Sebastian said.

"I don't know." Elanor frowned in puzzlement. "I don't think my father ever told me that."

"I'm sure it was the black one," Tom said.

"That makes sense," Quinn said. "Black is the color of darkness and death. It should be the color that unlocks a gate only ever opened in times of war."

"What does the white key open?" Elanor asked.

"I don't know," Quinn said. Her look of puzzlement deepened. "White is the color of light and revelation and life. You'd think it would open another gate, but there is no other that I know of, do you, Elanor?"

Elanor shook her head. "But I have discovered

many things I did not know about the castle these last few weeks."

Sebastian dragged over a bench and climbed onto it, reaching as high as he could. He could only just touch the end of the key with his fingertips. "I need another bench," he said.

"Careful," Elanor cautioned, as Tom helped him drag over another bench.

"Never," Sebastian replied with a grin. He climbed up onto the top bench, bracing a hand against the wall above the fireplace. He managed to unhook the black key and lowered it down to Tom. "Fungus, it's heavy!" he panted.

Tom and the girls caught the key and lowered it to the ground. It was as tall as Tom's shoulder.

"Its end is oddly shaped," Elanor said as Tom laid the key down on the floor. "Like a cross."

"That means the keyhole must be shaped like a cross, too," Quinn said.

"The white one is the same," Sebastian said, exerting all his strength to lift the white key down. They laid it down on the floor next to the black key.

Elanor sat back on her heels. "Look!"

Where the keys had hung above the mantelpiece was a cross-shaped hole. It had been hidden by the thick shafts of the two keys. The two heraldic beasts were both pointing towards the cross. "Could it . . . could it be a keyhole?" she asked, her voice shaking with sudden excitement.

"Maybe it opens a secret door—" Quinn caught her breath and could say no more.

"Only one way to find out!" Tom jumped up and heaved the white key.

Elanor was the lightest and so she clambered on top of the piled benches, the others holding her steady. Then Sebastian passed the key up to her. It took all her strength to get the key high enough to fit into the cross-shaped hole. It slid in smoothly, making them all grin in excitement and hope. Then Elanor took the end of the key in both her hands and twisted it with all her strength. A loud click rang out.

The back of the fireplace opened.

"It *is* a secret door!" Elanor cried, taking Sebastian's hand and jumping down to the ground.

Quinn bent and stepped inside the fireplace. She had to step over the ashes of the fire and suddenly remembered the strange rhyme the Grand Teller had spoken on the night of the midsummer feast.

"*By bone, over stone, through flame, out of ice, with breath, banish death*," Quinn chanted aloud. "We just opened the lock with a key made of bone that hung over stone." She put one hand on the stone and pushed gently. Silently the door swung open wider. "Now we need to step through the fireplace, where normally flames would be burning."

"Should we go in?" Elanor asked.

"Of course we should," Sebastian cried. "Let's hurry." He bent and stepped next to Quinn, looking into the dark maw of the passage revealed beyond.

"We'll need light." Tom gathered candlesticks from the high table. Sebastian lit the candles and one by one they crept in through the secret door. Fergus and Wulfric followed, ears pricked forward in interest.

"Wait a minute!" Tom stepped outside again and suddenly shut the door. He put his mouth to the stone. "Can you open the door from inside?"

A moment later, the door swung open. "What are you doing?" Sebastian cried.

"I don't want to leave the secret door open in case any guards come in searching for us," Tom said. "Here, help me put the keys back. We need to make it look as if we've never been in the hall."

He and Sebastian hung the two keys back in their usual spots, hiding the keyhole. They put the benches back where they had found them, then slipped back through the secret door, shutting it behind them. The girls were waiting impatiently, Wulfric and Fergus sitting by their sides. When Fergus waved his tail, it sent up a great cloud of choking dust.

"Come on!" Quinn cried. "Time's running out!"

For a moment, Tom stilled. Was this secret passage a wild-goose chase, leading them nowhere? Should they just give up and go in search of help?

But Sebastian was charging ahead. "Don't be an idiot," he said over his shoulder. "Don't you remember the Grand Teller's story? She said the heroes were under the Great Hall! And now we are too!"

11

SWORD IN ICE

"Look how thick the dust is," Elanor said. "No one has come this way in a very long time."

She coughed as the dust swirled up from her feet.

The passageway led steadily downward, slowly curving around in a spiral. The children followed it, trying hard not to send the dust swirling too high. Soon they reached a bitterly cold chamber. They shivered in their damp rags, rubbing their arms. Elanor lifted her candelabra high, but the flickering light of the candles barely pierced the shadows. They crept on. Slowly, their candles illuminated a gleaming block of ice.

Something golden curved out of it.

"It's a sword," said Sebastian. He gripped the golden hilt and tried to draw it out of the ice. It was stuck fast. "Fungus! That sword would have been really useful."

Tom tried, but the sword wouldn't budge. "Could we try to melt the ice?"

"If only Bel was here . . ." said Sebastian.

"Well, since she's not here, I guess we'll have to try it the old-fashioned way." They held their candle flames to the ice. Water dripped down. The ice gradually melted.

As the water dripped, it fell into a small basin at the base of the block of ice and then trickled away down a stone channel. Fergus and Wulfric lapped at it thirstily. The ice melted faster and faster. The sword began to reveal itself. Elanor had never seen a sword like it. It shone gold and had a wicked curve.

At last, Sebastian was able to draw the blade free of the ice, which broke apart and fell into the basin, sending a rush of water down the channel.

"Have you ever seen such a beautiful thing?" Sebastian exulted, sweeping the blade back and forth.

"It's so light, so perfectly balanced." As he whipped the sword around, it accidentally swiped off the top of Tom's candles, so that they were plunged into a deeper gloom. "So sharp," Sebastian marveled.

Tom rolled his eyes at Elanor and she bit back a grin. Nobody said anything to Sebastian, though.

"What's that noise?" Quinn interrupted.

They all fell silent, listening. A low rumble filled the air. Elanor lifted high her guttering candles.

A door of carved stone was grinding open a few steps ahead of them. "Look!" she pointed.

The water that had flowed down the channel was turning a waterwheel, and that in turn was opening the doors. The children rushed forward, Wulfric tumbling along behind.

Within was a beautifully wrought chamber, delicate pillars soaring high to a point in the center of the ceiling. Cobwebs were draped like gray tattered curtains from every height and covered four marble effigies that lay on raised tombstones. The statues' heads pointed towards the four points of the compass, while their feet faced a round basin in the very center of the room. As the water turned the wheel and opened the door, it ran on through a stone channel and poured into the dry-bottomed basin.

Two of the statues were men in chain mail and strange, pointed boots. One clasped a curved sword in his gauntleted hands, twin to the one in Sebastian's hands, though made of marble. The other had a longbow beside him, and a quiver full of stone arrows, all spun around with cobwebs.

The other two statues were women, their hair flowing to the floor like marble waterfalls. One had a stave of wood like a witch's staff in her hands; the other clasped the handle of a broken lance.

"They're just statues," Sebastian said. "Maybe the heroes are lying in those graves beneath them?"

It was a creepy idea. No one liked it at all.

"How do we wake them?" Elanor wondered.

"I guess we give them a shake and say 'wakey-wakey,'" Sebastian joked. But he did not step any closer to the four marble figures.

The children tiptoed farther into the room. The filthy cobwebs stirred from side to side and the dry leaves made a soft susurration on the marble floor. Tom gazed around and saw that a window casement was set in the far wall. Faint light seeped in through the window, and he could see that the horizon was touched with warm color.

"The sun is rising," Quinn said. "We were supposed to bring together the four ingredients at dawn. We have to hurry!" She held the sea serpent scale before her like a round silver shield. Elanor held the black unicorn's horn and Sebastian grasped the dragon tooth. Tom drew out the golden griffin feathers.

"*When the wolf lies down with the wolfhound and the stones of the castle sing, the sleeping heroes shall wake for the crown and the bells of victory ring,*" Quinn chanted. "Well, the wolf is lying down with the wolfhound." She nodded at Fergus and Wulfric, lying peacefully together by the pillar. "But how are we to make the stones of the castle sing?"

"Stones can't sing," Sebastian said.

"Always thinking so literally," Quinn mocked him gently. "Ever heard of a metaphor, Sebastian?"

"Well, yes, but I have no idea what it means,"

he retorted.

Quinn opened her mouth to enlighten him, but Tom had been inspecting the room while they argued and now he cried, "Look!"

A curved hunting horn hung from the pillar on a chain. It was so gray and furred with dust, it was almost invisible among all the draping cobwebs.

Tom reached for it and Quinn nodded. "Remember, Arwen said, 'with breath, banish death . . .' That must be what she meant. We need to blow the horn to wake the sleeping heroes."

"You do it," Elanor said to Tom.

Tom gingerly unhooked the horn and blew off the dust and cobwebs. A warm gleam revealed itself. "It's made of gold!" he cried.

He turned it upside down and shook it, then cleaned the ivory mouthpiece with the tail of his shirt. Outside the window, the sky was tinted rose and amber, and Tom could hear birds twittering. "Shall I do it?"

The others all nodded, breathless with nervous excitement.

Tom lifted the horn to his mouth and blew with all the air in his lungs. A wild, high note rang out. It resonated all around the chamber, building to a crescendo that echoed and echoed until it seemed as if the whole castle hummed with music.

Elanor, Quinn and Sebastian watched in awe.

"*And the stones of the castle sing*,'" Quinn quoted softly.

"There!" Elanor pointed with a shaking hand.

The eyes of the statues had opened, gleaming with bright and human life.

STATUES ← ← ←
» → COME TO LIFE

Tom gazed, openmouthed, as the statues stirred and moved.

One of the men stretched wide his arms, yawning. Dust fell from him in a cloud, showing the metal of his chain mail beneath.

The woman with the broken lance rolled onto her side, yawning. She sat up slowly, dust cascading away from her. "Art thou awake, Sir Geraint?" she said.

"That I am, Lady Rhianwyn," the man with the longbow answered, sitting up. He shook his head, then sneezed as dust and webs fell around him in a white shower. "I wish the Grand Teller had devised some way to ward away the spiders."

The woman with the dagger had also sat up and was shaking her dress. Pale-winged moths fluttered out from the fabric.

"'Tis good to see thee, Mistress Ifanna," Lady Rhianwyn murmured with a smile. She turned to Sir Geraint. "The spell does not stop spiders from weaving their webs. Time for us was only slowed, not stopped."

Sir Geraint stood up, brushing himself off vigorously. He sent up such a storm of dust that Tom sneezed. At once, all four warriors turned and gazed at the children.

"Who is it that disturbs our rest?" boomed the man with the sword.

"Speak gently, Lord Vaughn," the other woman said. "Canst thou not see they are but children?"

"I beg your pardon, sir." Elanor dropped into a graceful curtsey. "We have woken you at a time of terrible need."

"What then is thy need?" Lady Rhianwyn asked, dusting off her skirt.

"Wolfhaven Castle has been invaded by enemies that use dark sorcery to further their aims. We need to defeat them and rescue our people from the dungeons."

"Hast thou brought us gifts?" Sir Geraint asked.

Elanor stepped forward, holding up the black unicorn's horn. "We have."

"I thank thee." Lady Rhianwyn fitted the horn into the end of the broken lance. It slotted into place perfectly, turning into a formidable-looking weapon. She then dipped the point of the horn into the water in the fountain. It glittered silver.

"Hast thou a gift for me?" Mistress Ifanna asked.

Quinn held out the sea serpent scale. Mistress Ifanna thanked her and fitted the mother-of-pearl scale over her arm like a shield. She looked stern and magnificent, her witch's staff in one hand and the shield guarding the other.

Tom stepped forward next, holding out the griffin feathers. "I thank thee," Sir Geraint answered with a smile as he took them from Tom's hand. "I shall be able to fletch my arrows again." He unslung the quiver from his back and deftly used a small knife to trim the griffin feathers into shape, fitting them into place at the end of each arrow.

Sebastian held out the dragon tooth. Lord Vaughn inclined his head unsmilingly and took it from his hand. "'Tis rather small," he said, turning it in his gauntleted hands.

"It's from a baby dragon," Sebastian explained.

Lord Vaughn grunted. "I thank thee for thy gift, and promise to use it wisely." He attached the dragon tooth to a leather cord around his neck.

Sir Geraint was expertly fixing the feathers to his arrows. They gleamed golden in the growing light. When each arrow was fletched to his satisfaction, he turned to Tom and said, "Give me thy horn."

Reluctantly, Tom handed it over. He had felt such a moment of thrilling excitement when he had blown the horn, as if he had shaken off his own carapace of stone and was at last who he was meant to be, a boy with music singing through every pulse of his blood, every spark of his nerves.

"Prepare thyselves," Sir Geraint instructed the others. The four warriors gripped their weapons tight. Then Sir Geraint lifted the horn to his mouth and blew a great blast.

A wind sprang up from nowhere, swirling around the room and lifting away every leaf and cobweb and every particle of dust. Tom staggered and grasped at a pillar to keep his feet. Elanor was blown right over and had to be helped up by Sebastian. Quinn's black curls were blown sideways like a rippling banner. Fergus's shaggy coat gusted backward, his ears turning inside out. Wulfric tumbled head over heels. Tom had never felt such a wind. It stung and prickled till his skin was tingling with pins and needles. Then, the black whirlwind swept out the window.

The four warriors were as clean and fresh as if they had never been covered with hundreds of years of dust and cobwebs. Mistress Ifanna's dress proved to be white, while Lady Rhianwyn's hair shone golden brown. Lord Vaughn's hair and beard were fiery red, while Sir Geraint's eyes were as blue as forget-me-nots. Wonderingly Tom realized that his own tattered clothes were now as fresh and clean as if they were new.

One by one, the four warriors stepped up to the fountain at the center of the room and, using a golden cup that had hung there unseen, drank from the water

that glimmered within. It seemed to give them new strength. Lady Rhianwyn stood straighter, her eyes shining with vigor. The lines around Lord Vaughn's mouth disappeared. Mistress Ifanna laughed. "Is it not good to be awake once more?" she cried.

When Sir Geraint had drunk his fill, he beckoned the children forward. One by one, they drank. It was like no water Tom had ever tasted. It was cold, yet shot through his body like fire. It was sweet like honey, but scintillated as if stars had been melted in it. He had been hungry, tired and afraid, but the water made his whole body thrill with new energy.

Sebastian was just bending to dip in the cup when he looked up in sudden doubt. "Drinking this water will not enchant us into being sleeping heroes, will it?"

"Knave!" Lord Vaughn shouted. "Dost thou dare accuse us of such base treachery?"

"Peace, Lord Vaughn," Mistress Ifanna soothed. "He means no disrespect. No, my dear boy." She smiled at Sebastian, who turned red all the way to the tips of his ears. "The water will give thee strength and courage. One can only be bound to such a spell as ours with a willing heart and a true wish to serve."

"I . . . I was just checking," he stammered and drank down a cupful rapidly.

Tom gazed at the four stern-faced heroes in amazement. It was incredible to think these four men and women had all chosen to have such a spell cast upon them. They had slept hidden under the castle for hundreds of years, waiting till they were needed to rise and fight. What had they left behind? Who had mourned them? What had they sacrificed to keep Wolfhaven Castle safe?

"We can only fight till sunset," Lady Rhianwyn told the children. "As the last light fades, we must be back in our chamber, else we shall turn to dust on the battlefield and blow away, lost forever."

"Let us fight till sunset then!" Sir Geraint cried, and led the way out of the chamber at a run.

13

MAD MOB-BALL

"Valor, glory, victory!" Sebastian shouted, waving his new sword. The curved blade flashed golden in the bright sunrise. He sprinted after the four warriors, Quinn and Tom close behind, the wolfhound and the wolf cub at their heels.

Elanor filled her leather bottle with water from the stone basin. Her father and the other prisoners may be in need of its healing powers, too.

Tom, Quinn and Sebastian were busy hauling down the black key when she finally joined them in the Great Hall.

"Let's go open the war gate!" Tom said. "Then we'll need weapons."

"I have a sword," Sebastian said, brandishing it joyfully. "I'll go and find Beltaine. I hope she hasn't been hurt."

"I hope Sabre's all right, too," Quinn admitted.

"And Quickthorn," Elanor said. "And I must find my father!"

"I can't wait to see Mam," Tom said. "We must rescue them first. Let's go!"

Half running, they carried the heavy key between them, out the far doors and into the inner ward.

Outside was chaos. Lord Mortlake's knights fought with the four warriors who stood back-to-back, an island of color in a sea of black. Slowly they were forced towards the southern end of the inner ward, where the old keep stood above the family crypt. Bog-men scuttled from every door and gateway, their desiccated faces and bodies more hideous than ever in the fresh dawn light. It seemed impossible that two men and two women could possibly withstand such a force. And yet they all fought with incredible strength and determination, each creating a clear circle around them.

Finally the four warriors were backed up to the heavy oak door that led into the family crypt where generations of lords and ladies of Wolfhaven were buried. The other three feinted and parried as Lord Vaughn pulled the door open. Then he pulled out the dragon tooth and tossed it into the crypt.

Stone grated on stone. A smell of damp rolled out. Then out marched a regiment of skeletons, dressed in tattered robes. Most wore coronets on their bare skulls and carried rusting swords. A few were mounted on the skeletons of horses, with skeleton dogs at their heels. A bluish light hung around them, as if they carried some remnant of spirit within.

Sir Geraint blew the golden horn.

"Attack!" Lady Rhianwyn shouted.

The skeleton army charged.

Many of the black-armored knights broke ranks and fled. Elanor could hardly blame them.

Lord Vaughn swept around him with his golden sword, taking off the heads of a dozen bog-men at once. Lady Rhianwyn vaulted up onto the back of a horse's skeleton and charged the knights with her unicorn horn lance. Sir Geraint shot a gleaming fire of gold-feathered arrows with deadly aim, while Mistress Ifanna fought with her staff and shield.

"You carry the key, I'll guard your backs," Sebastian said, sword at the ready.

"Me too." Tom drew his dagger.

The girls hurried down the inner ward, carrying the key between them. Sebastian and Tom ran behind them, the wolfhound snarling and leaping upon any knights that got too close. The wolf cub snapped at the heels of the bog-men, tangling in their legs so they tripped and fell. They reached the northern gatehouse, with its long arched passageway that led through to the barbican and the gate to the outside world.

Together, Quinn and Elanor raced through the crowd to the gate. Someone swiped a sword at Elanor's head and she ducked, her heart racing faster than a warhorse at full gallop. All around her metal clanged, men shouted and arrows whined.

"This is like the maddest game of mob-ball ever," Sebastian panted. "Come on, get that gate open!"

The lock was too high for them to reach. Quinn pushed the key into Elanor's arms. "I'll lift you up. Quick!" With all her strength, Quinn heaved her up and Elanor managed to get the key into the cross-shaped keyhole. The lock clicked open.

"Open the gate," Tom shouted. Wulfric jumped up and fastened his teeth into a bog-man's leathery posterior. He was shaken from side to side, all four paws off the ground. With a sound of tearing leather, the flap of skin ripped free and Wulfric somersaulted one way and the bog-man another.

Elanor and Quinn together dragged the massive gate forward. Sebastian sprang to their aid.

"Watch out!" Tom shouted. "They've got boiling oil ready to pour!"

Elanor glanced up. Knights were lifting steaming vats to the murder holes that pierced the stone wall of the gatehouse. Elanor could hear the oil spitting and hissing. They began to pour. Hot yellow liquid rained down on the courtyard. Men screamed.

"Come on!" Sebastian shouted.

The gate opened and they sprang through.

"Fergus!" Tom yelled. The wolfhound streaked past them, his ears blown back, his long tongue flapping. Wulfric raced at his heels, yelping as a splash of hot oil landed on his plumy tail.

The boiling oil streamed into the courtyard.

"We need to rescue the prisoners now, come on!" Elanor called.

"I have to see if Sabre is alive! I'll rouse the town." Quinn began to race down the road towards the town.

"I'll ring the bells!" Tom cried.

"Meet us at the dungeons!" Sebastian shouted.

Tom nodded and raced towards the inner ward, the wolfhound swift and gray at his heels, Wulfric scrambling to keep up. In a moment, he was gone.

"We should hide the key," Elanor panted. "Else they'll just close and lock the gate again."

"Where?" Sebastian asked.

Knights were racing down the steps from the

barbican, now slicked with hot oil. The only clear path was back through the passageway and into the inner ward. "To the kitchens!" Elanor cried. "There's a passage there that leads down into the dungeons."

Sebastian and Elanor carried the key. The clatter of metallic boots came up fast behind them. The knights were after them.

"I'll keep them off. Can you carry the key yourself?" Without waiting for an answer, Sebastian shoved the key into Elanor's arms and spun to face the knights racing towards them, his sword swinging.

Elanor staggered on alone. The key was so heavy. Her arms ached and she could scarcely snatch a breath. She came to the end of the passageway and slipped around the edges of the wall. No one in the inner ward noticed her, all too busy fighting the army of skeletons. Lord Vaughn was doing battle with Lord Mortlake, his curved sword flashing. Lord Mortlake fought like a madman. He had lost his helmet and his teeth were bared in a grimace. Sweat poured down his face. He came at Lord Vaughn with his sword swinging so violently, the red-bearded man was knocked off his feet. Lord Mortlake's sword hacked down, but Lord Vaughn rolled and leapt back up.

The sound of frantic neighing came from the stables. Elanor paused, wondering if it was Quickthorn she heard. She saw knights racing towards her from the watchtower, and at once began to heave the key as fast as she could towards the kitchen. She could not risk being captured.

At last she reached the kitchen door, which was locked. Elanor gulped, and glanced back over her shoulder. Sir Geraint shot down four knights who had been racing towards her. He saluted her and bounded away. Elanor took a deep breath and banged on the door. "Let me in! Please! It's me, Lady Elanor. Please let me in."

The door suddenly opened. A young woman looked out, her face terrified. "Help me," Elanor pleaded. They dragged the key in over the threshold together and slammed the door shut and locked and bolted it. Seconds later, knights were beating on the door with their sword hilts.

"Help me hide it," Elanor cried. She remembered

the secret passageway that led from the larder and began to drag the key that way.

"But where? What's happening? Have we been attacked?" The young woman had a round rosy face and round brown eyes. Wisps of brown curls escaped from under her white cap.

"We were attacked over three weeks ago," Elanor told her. "By Lord Mortlake. Now we're fighting back."

"But—"

"I have no time to explain. You just need to trust me. What's your name?"

"Sophie. I'm the new cook," she gabbled.

"Did you never wonder what happened to the old cook?" Elanor was grimly dragging the key across the flagstones, all too aware of the banging on the door.

"Well . . . no." Sophie helped her, her face growing flushed at the exertion.

"She's locked up in the dungeon, along with my father and the castle men-at-arms!"

"What? Lord Wolfgang is in the dungeon?" Sophie's eyes rounded with horror.

"Yes. I have to rescue him. Please, I'll need your

help." Elanor's breath was coming short and fast, and she felt her arms were being dragged out of their sockets. At last they reached the larder and Sophie helped Elanor drag the key inside.

"Quick, shut the door." Elanor could hear the wood of the kitchen door cracking.

She rushed to the back of the small room, clambering over barrels, and pressed a small stone near the floor. With a click, the latch released and the wooden wall of the larder swung open. "Help me get the key in." Elanor pulled at the key and Sophie rushed to lift its base. Together, they managed to maneuver the enormous key over the barrels and into the secret passage within.

"But I thought you and your father were unwell," Sophie whispered. "I thought you were both resting while Lord Mortlake ran things for you. Is he not to be your father-in-law?"

"It's all lies. I'm only twelve; I'm not marrying anyone. And when I do, you can be sure I won't be marrying a Mortlake! While everyone here's been under a spell of mist, we've been running and fighting and trying to get help to defeat that villain!" Elanor heard the door to the kitchen crash open and put her finger to her lips. "I'm going to hide in the secret passage," she whispered. "I need you to tell the knights that I've gone up the staircase to the Lady's Tower. Then take a basket of food and a jug of pear cider to the guards in the dungeon. Put some valerian or poppy in it to make them sleep."

"Oh, but I couldn't." Sophie shrank back.

"Of course you can! Please, Sophie, I need you to be brave and help me. Wolfhaven depends upon it."

The kitchen door burst open.

Elanor clambered through to the secret passage and shut the door on Sophie's round, frightened face.

A moment later, she heard an angry man's voice. "The girl who just ran in here! Where is she?"

Sophie, quavering, terrified, pointed. "She . . . she went through there!"

14

»—→FIREBALL←—«

Sebastian fought the knights with all his strength. He was just one boy against half a dozen grown men, though. He had to find another advantage.

He ducked under one knight's sword, kicked another hard behind the knee, then ran for the steps that led up into the guardhouse. The knights pursued him, as he had hoped. Sebastian bounded up the stairs as fast as he could. He reached the first level and raced along the corridor. A few vats had been left near the murder holes, and Sebastian kicked them over. The knights slipped and fell.

Sebastian ran for the guardroom in the Black Tower and locked the door behind him. Grabbing a leather sack, he began to shove weapons inside it. Swords, daggers, flails, maces. His heart was racing. With the sack slung over his shoulder, Sebastian ran towards the Lady's Tower. The kitchen was on the lowest floor of that tower and he hoped to find Elanor there.

Why haven't the warning bells rung? he frantically thought. *Surely Tom should have reached the bell tower by now?*

Sebastian came through to the courtyard, which was lined with barrels and piled high with bales of straw. He could hear the sounds of battle from the inner ward and caught a quick glimpse of Lord Vaughn and Lady Rhianwyn fighting back-to-back. An ocean of bog-men broke upon them.

Somewhere nearby a horse neighed, pounding its hooves against the wooden walls of its stable. Sebastian wondered if it could be Quickthorn, locked in the stable. Would Beltaine be nearby, too? With a sharp twist of anxiety, he decided he had to creep into the stables and see if he could free the unicorn and find his dragon.

Hefting the heavy sack higher on his back, Sebastian crept around the shadowy edges of the courtyard. A flicker of movement caught the corner of his eye. To his horror, a group of bog-men had crept in through the gateway. They all carried long spears in their leathery hands and were sniffing the air, their sightless eyes turning this way and that.

Sebastian froze. The weapons in the sack clanked. At once, the hideous, sunken faces of the bog-men snapped towards him. They leapt forward, spears at the ready.

Sebastian took to his heels, the bog-men close behind. He knocked over a barrel with one foot and it broke, spilling foul-smelling liquid in the bog-men's path. Sebastian recognized the stench of saltpeter. It was the flammable liquid into which Lord Mortlake's knights dipped their arrows. Sebastian knew that the bog-men were terrified of fire. He could create a wall of fire between him and the bog-men.

But how was he to light the fire?

"Oh, Bel, if only you were here to breathe sparks on it!" he cried.

The bog-men advanced on him, spears held high. He had only a few seconds. Sebastian ran, slashing at barrels every step of the way, then scrambled atop the bales of straw. He threw down the sack of weapons, dropped his sword and rummaged in his pack for the tinderbox. Urgently, he struck his steel against his flint. His hands were shaking so badly, he could not strike a spark. Sebastian took a deep breath, steadied his nerves and struck again. A spray of sparks shot out and landed in the straw. Red filaments writhed out. Sebastian puffed till tiny flames flickered up. He gathered up the burning handful of straw and threw it with all his strength into the courtyard. Then he grabbed the sack and his sword and jumped as far as he could in the opposite direction.

WHUMP! A giant fireball ignited in the courtyard. Burning bog-men were flung in all directions. Sebastian felt the blast of heat at his back, but did not look back. He ran as fast as his legs could carry him through the door and into the stable.

Horses were rearing in terror in their stalls. Smoke billowed through the door as Sebastian slammed it shut and dropped the bolt in place, then ran down the center aisle opening all the stalls and letting the horses flee in panic.

To his joy, he found Quickthorn confined within the stall closest to the stable doors. The unicorn was hobbled and bound in chains. Sebastian struggled to set the horned beast free. He could hear the roar of the fire getting closer. Smoke stung his eyes. At last he undid the final buckle and the unicorn reared. Sebastian fell back as Quickthorn galloped out of the stall and into the melee.

Sebastian hauled up the sack of weapons again, grabbed his sword and ran. His legs felt like lead, his eyes swam, his throat burned. He saw the doorway like an oblong of brightness against the black smoke. Summoning all his strength, he lurched out the door, then fell to his knees, coughing violently.

Only when his coughing at last subsided did he realize that he had fallen before the steel boots of Lord Mortlake.

15

LADIES DO NOT SKULK

Quinn ran through the streets of the town, shouting till her voice was hoarse. "The castle is under attack! Beware! Enemies in the castle!"

People hurried from every house. They all looked pale and sick. Quinn could not imagine what it must have been like living in the mist for almost a month, breathing its poisonous fumes.

"Are you sure?" a man asked.

"The bells have not rung out," a woman protested.

Tom, where are you? Quinn thought. *Why haven't you rung the bells?*

"Lord Mortlake has seized control of the castle. Please help!" Shouting all the way, Quinn ran on.

She reached the harbor front. The prow of the broken warship pointed up at the noon sun. She hoped desperately that Tom had not been captured. Her heart constricted as if squeezed between giant hands. Perhaps all her friends had been caught. Perhaps the awakened warriors had been defeated. Perhaps she was all alone in her quest to save the castle.

Tears flooded down her face and her voice grew so desperate that people stopped arguing with her and went to grab what weapons they could—frying pans, rolling pins, hayforks and fire shovels. It gladdened Quinn's heart to see burly butchers and bakers and candlestick makers taking up arms and marching on the castle.

But still there was no sign of Sabre. Quinn could only hope that her sea serpent had fled to the safety of the open sea. Yet she felt sure that the great beast would not go till she had bid it farewell. She had saved Sabre's life and the sea serpent was somehow bound to her. *Please do not let him have been killed*, she prayed.

Quinn stood on the wharf and looked out across the harbor. Most of the boats had been broken and destroyed, and the shipping yard had been laid to waste. She shivered, thinking of the terror the sailors must have felt with a sea serpent on the rampage within the harbor.

The moon was low in the sky, no thicker than a thread of spun sugar. Tonight there would be no moon at all. The night of the dark moon was the best time for casting spells of black magic. She had to stop Lady Mortlake and Mistress Mauldred before they cast any more death curses.

A flutter of dark draperies caught her eye. An old hunchbacked woman was hobbling away from the harbor, leaning on a tall staff. Giant rats ran before her and after her. Goose bumps rose on Quinn's skin.

It was Wilda of the Witchwood, who had betrayed Quinn and her friends.

Quinn gripped her own staff tightly, wondering what she should do. Wilda was a powerful sorceress and Quinn was afraid to confront her on her own. For a moment, she found it impossible to move.

Then she saw that Wilda carried a jar with a wire handle. As she shuffled along, water sloshed out of the jar. Something small was wriggling inside, something small and silvery black. Quinn frowned. A dreadful certainty came over her. She began to run towards the old witch. The closer Quinn came to her, the more certain she became.

Wilda had shrunk Sabre to the size of a sardine.

Furious, Quinn broke into a run. The giant rats saw her racing towards them and began to squeak loudly. Wilda looked up, recognition flashing across her face. She turned and hurried inside the gateway to the cemetery. It had not been tended in months, and thistles and weeds grew high. Brambles clambered over the tombstones.

Wilda turned to face Quinn, her staff set firmly on the bare earth.

"That's my sea serpent," Quinn cried. "You've shrunk him!"

"He was making a nuisance of himself," Wilda said.

"Let him go," Quinn demanded, barely able to contain herself. "Restore him to his normal size."

"And just how will you make me do that?" Wilda sneered. "A mere witch apprentice like you?"

Quinn bit her lip, tears stinging her eyes. As she hesitated, Wilda brought up her own witch's staff and rapped Quinn sharply across the forehead.

"Quick as a wink, make her shrink," she said.

And Quinn did.

Elanor crept along the shadowy corridor.

She had hidden the key in one of the cellars and then waited as long as she dared for Sophie to do as she'd promised. Elanor had hoped that Tom or Sebastian would come to find her as they'd planned. But neither had turned up and Elanor had still not heard the warning bells ring. This troubled her greatly. Eventually, she could not bear the suspense any longer.

She was just about to tiptoe towards the dungeons when a heavy hand fell upon her shoulder. A huge ring flashed sullen red fire. Elanor jumped and gave a little scream.

"Lady Elanor, what on earth are you doing skulking around down here?" Mistress Mauldred said. "Ladies do not skulk."

Sebastian was hauled to his feet by a steel gauntlet.

"Got you!" Lord Mortlake said.

He was so strong that Sebastian hung in the air like a kitten being carried by its mother.

Despair washed over him. He had been so close!

Instead, he dangled in the air like a fool.

"And you thought you could be a knight," Lord Mortlake jeered. "A clumsy idiot like you! No wonder your father sent you away. He couldn't bear to see his only son tripping over his own feet all the time."

Sebastian struggled to get free.

"Where are the rest of you?" Lord Mortlake demanded.

Sebastian shrugged. Lord Mortlake hit him across the ear with his other hand, making Sebastian's head ring. "I honestly don't know. We got separated."

Lord Mortlake dropped him, and Sebastian sprawled at his feet again. He got up, glancing around him quickly.

Black smoke billowed from the burning stable. Men ran back and forth from the kitchen well, carrying buckets of water to try and put it out. Sebastian smiled grimly. At least he had caused a grand kerfuffle.

Meanwhile, the inner ward was a scene of utter chaos. Runaway horses reared and bucked, trampling the knights trying to catch them. Bog-men lay in smoking piles. Sir Geraint was shooting swift golden-fletched arrows from the shelter of the crypt, while Quickthorn fought side by side with Lady Rhianwyn upon the bony back of the skeleton horse. Lady Rhianwyn's black-tipped lance plunged and twirled and struck again and again. Lord Vaughn and Mistress Ifanna stood back-to-back, guarding each other as they fought. His sword flashed golden through the smoke, her shield was like a spinning wheel of light. The skeleton army fought on tirelessly, rusty swords clanging, beating the bog-men back.

But it was not nearly enough. They were surrounded on all sides by the relentless advance of bog-men. Thousands of them. And they were hard to kill. If Lord Vaughn chopped off their sticklike arms and legs, they simply crawled on, like spiders whose limbs had been torn off. If Sir Geraint shot them full of arrows, they simply plucked them out and kept on scuttling. The four heroes were tiring, and still the ranks of bog-men pressed on.

"We have only to fight till sunset, then those heroes of yours will turn to dust and be no more trouble to us," Lord Mortlake said with satisfaction. "It is already past noon. We need only hold them off a half a dozen more hours, then they'll be gone."

Sebastian could see the sun, an orange disk burning through the smoke. Lord Mortlake was right. It was already sliding down towards the bell tower, which stood on the western wall facing the sea. He had been running and fighting for hours.

"And once the sun is gone, it will be the night of the dark moon and the best time for dark magic," Lord Mortlake said. "You think you have thwarted us. Trust me, all you have done is slow us for a few hours."

"Your warship is smashed to smithereens," Sebastian pointed out.

Lord Mortlake scowled. "I can build another."

"Your magical mist is all blown away and Quinn is down there now, rousing the townsfolk against you."

Lord Mortlake's frown deepened, but he shrugged. "The time for subterfuge may be over, anyway. Tonight my wife and her sister shall cast a curse on the king and he shall die. I'll be king by tomorrow, and there's nothing you or anyone else can do to stop me."

16

QUICK →← AS A WINK

Elanor could not speak nor hardly breathe. Terror paralyzed her.

"I'm very glad to have you in hand again." Mistress Mauldred dug her fingers into Elanor's shoulder. "You have been unforgivably meddlesome. What *would* your mother think?"

Elanor gritted her teeth.

"No doubt you think to rescue your fool of a father. I'm sure you were looking forward to weeping all over each other. Well, it does not suit me to have your father blundering around and getting in my way. That is, if he had the strength to blunder." She laughed. "A month in a dungeon has an admirable way of weakening a man."

"I want to see him," Elanor cried.

"Of course you do. But I'm afraid it'll be a while before you see anyone. A few solitary days without food or water and we'll see how your manners improve."

She marched forward, pushing Elanor along before her. The doorway at the far end of the room was locked and barred, with a big ring of keys hanging on a hook nearby. As she unlocked the door, Mistress Mauldred gripped Elanor's shoulder tightly like an iron vice. Then, carrying the ring of keys in her other hand, she shoved Elanor hard through the door.

Elanor stumbled, but regained her balance quickly. She lifted her head high and said, "Mistress Mauldred, don't you know? Ladies do not shove."

Her governess was taken aback. For a moment, she did not speak, then color rose on her cheekbones.

Mistress Mauldred sailed on down a narrow corridor, lined on either side by heavy iron doors. She unlocked one, which swung open, revealing a cramped stone room filled with foul-smelling straw. There was no chair or table or bed or chamber pot.

"In you go," Mistress Mauldred ordered.

"Ladies first," Elanor said with a demure curtsey and a sweeping gesture of one hand.

Mistress Mauldred gave a pinched, superior smile and swept into the cell.

At once, Elanor slammed the door and turned the key in the lock. Her governess at once began to shriek and hammer her fists on the iron door.

Elanor tutted. "Now, now, Mistress Mauldred. Ladies do not have temper tantrums."

Quinn reeled back, dizzy and sick, her skin prickling all over with pins and needles as she shrunk at an incredible rate. The world rushed up past her eyes, everything growing bigger and bigger. Wilda looked like a gnarled and ancient oak tree, towering over her. The rats swarming towards her were as big as oxen, their sharp yellow teeth like swinging scythes. In a second, they would be upon her.

Quinn jammed her staff through her sash, then caught hold of Wilda's hem and swung out of the way of the lunging rats. Hand over hand, she hauled herself up. Two enormous pincer fingers tried to seize her, but Quinn was too quick and nimble.

She found the end of the witch's dangling sash and swung back and forth, gaining height before somersaulting up to catch hold of one of the witch's necklaces. Up Quinn climbed, then leapt to catch hold of one of the long gray locks of hair which hung over the witch's shoulders.

She swung away from Wilda's head. As she swayed past the witch's huge face, each wrinkle etched like a deep canyon, Quinn reached out with her staff and knocked the witch hard between the eyes.

"Quick as a wink, make her shrink!" Quinn cried, then let go.

She tumbled down helplessly, head over heels, but gripped tightly to her staff so she would not drop it. As she fell, the witch shrank beside her.

Quinn landed in the thick black fur of a rat, then rolled off. As soon as her bare feet touched the ground, she banged the staff as hard as she could, shouting, "I'm too small, make me tall!"

Up she shot, growing a foot a second. Soon, the houses and shops of Wolfhaven Town only reached her knee. Clouds whirled around her head.

"I'm scraping the skies," she boomed in panic. "Make me the right size."

Down she shrank, till she was the perfect Quinn size. The giant rats rushed at her, but she knocked her staff on the ground and said wearily, "Begone rats, else I'll conjure cats."

The giant rats turned and raced away. Quinn was left sitting on the ground, with a tiny witch jumping up and down at her knee and trying to hit her with a staff no bigger than a thistledown.

Wilda had dropped the jar when she had begun to shrink, and it now lay on its side in the mud. Quinn carefully tipped the jar so the tiny sea serpent could slither out into the puddle. Quinn leaned forward and very gently touched the tiny snake with the head of her staff. "Nice and slow, make Sabre grow," she said.

And he did.

Quinn shook out the last few drops of water, then picked up the tiny witch by the neck of her robe and gently dropped her into the jar.

"That should keep you out of trouble for a while!"

Sebastian tensed, balancing on the balls of his feet. He was so angry, it was like a red mist hung before his eyes.

"Where's my dragon?" he demanded.

Lord Mortlake laughed. "Quite a bad-tempered little thing, isn't it? It tried to bite my hand so I had it locked in the hanging cage."

He waved his hand towards the bell tower. Sebastian squinted through the smoke. He could just see a small cage, hanging by a chain from the tower's battlements. Beltaine was cramped within, the iron bars pressing cruelly into her body. Her wings were all bent flat, and her tail was squashed around her neck. She was crying piteously.

"You . . . you fiend!" Sebastian burst into a run and

tackled Lord Mortlake, knocking him backward. Lord Mortlake hit the ground with a smack.

Then Sebastian ran straight through the skirmish. Bog-men tried to catch him, but he ducked, weaved and sidestepped straight through their outstretched hands and towards the bell tower. "You leathery things should learn to play mob-ball!" he shouted.

Elanor rushed to the door of the main dungeon and unlocked it with shaking hands. As the door swung open, the prisoners all cringed away from the light, shielding their eyes. Elanor saw many faces she recognized, but she kept looking frantically for her father. At last she found him, pale and hollow cheeked.

He rose to his feet, holding out trembling hands.

"Ela?"

"Father!"

She embraced him lovingly, shocked at the feel of his ribs through his robe.

"You're safe," he murmured, stroking her hair. "I've been so afraid for you."

"And I for you."

"Where have you been? What's happening?"

"We've awakened the sleeping heroes of legend, Father, just like Arwen told us to!" She heard a cry of gladness and turned to see the old witch clasping her hands together in joy.

"I knew you could do it," Arwen said. "Brave of heart, sharp of wit, strong of spirit and steadfast of purpose, as you all are!"

"I have so much to tell you, but not here, not now," Elanor said. "There'll be knights back very soon and we must be gone by then. Here, drink a mouthful of this, Father, then pass it along. It will give you strength."

He drank, then passed the leather bottle along to Arwen. As she drank, the old witch straightened her bent back and the lines of sorrow and fear faded from her face. Everyone in the cell drank, then passed the bottle back to Elanor. There was still some water left inside, so she stoppered it carefully and hung it at her belt, knowing it would be useful at the end of the battle.

"Let's get you to safety," she said. "Those who are too sick or old can hide in the secret passage. The rest must come and help us fight for the castle."

"I shall fight!" cried Sir Kevyn.

"And I! And I!" cried many more voices.

"So shall I," Lord Wolfgang said, standing tall in his filthy, tattered robe. "I am the lord of this castle and I shall fight for my people."

Elanor gazed at him, marveling. Despite his emaciated frame and grimy face, he looked more alive than she ever remembered seeing him. Was it the enchanted water? Or perhaps the spell Mistress Mauldred had cast over him had finally been broken?

"Sebastian has gone to find weapons," she said. "And Tom will be ringing the warning bells any minute now, to call in help from the town and the countryside."

Except the bells had not rung.

Tom drifted slowly into consciousness.

His shoulder hurt. So did his head. It was freezing.

Tom opened his eyes groggily. All was dark. For an awful, frantic moment, he thought he had been blinded. A dim light was filtering down from overhead. Far above was a small bright circle of light.

Memory began to return. He tried to sit up. Water surged around him, splashing his face. Tom realized he was lying half in, half out, of water. Something hard was beneath him, cutting into his armpit and his stomach. Then he remembered.

Lady Mortlake had thrown him down the well.

He had been running, full speed, from the

gatehouse towards the bell tower. If he rang the bells, his father would come. Perhaps the whole countryside would rise to defend the castle.

He had heard a thunder of hooves behind him. He had glanced over one shoulder.

Hurtling towards him was the giant boar, yellow tusks curving up from either side of its snout. On its broad and bristly back rode Lady Mortlake, her black hair whipping out behind her. Her lips were drawn into a snarl and her eyes were lit with madness.

Tom tried to bolt for the cover of the garden, but in seconds she was upon him. She seized him by the hair and somehow dragged him up onto the boar in front of her. Tom tried to jerk free, but she had too tight a grip on him.

"I've had enough of you and your troublesome friends," she had hissed. "It's time to get rid of you once and for all."

With a skid, the giant boar drew up in front of the knights' well, set in the corner under the stairs that led up to the bell tower. Tom fell heavily, banging his elbow on the paving stones. Lady Mortlake hauled him over to the well. He tried to break free, but it felt like she was ripping out every hair on his head.

"Well, you won't be troubling me anymore." With unbelievable strength she had lifted him and hurled him down the well.

I must have hit my head on the way down, Tom thought. He felt cautiously around him. His fall had been broken by the big wooden bucket. He was lying half across it, his legs dangling in the water. They were numb with cold.

He looked back up at the circle of light above him.

What had happened to Fergus? And Wulfric? The last Tom had seen, they had been running behind him. Had Lady Mortlake killed them?

And his friends? Had they been caught too?

He had to get out. He groped along the wall. His head swam. Gritting his teeth, Tom put one foot in a crack and heaved himself up. His muscles protested.

Slowly, laboriously, he climbed out of the well.

When he finally crawled out of the well mouth, his arms and legs trembled uncontrollably and his hands were torn and bleeding. He collapsed onto the paving stones, trying to catch his breath.

Smoke drifted everywhere, the dark shapes of fighting men looming up, then being obscured again. It was hard to tell what time it was, for the sun was nigh invisible behind the clouds of black smoke. The light was strange and reddish. He could hear a shrill whinnying, the clash of arms and the pound of running feet.

Then Sebastian hurtled past him, the golden sword in one hand. He came out of the smoke so unexpectedly and flashed past so fast that Tom barely had time to call out. Lord Mortlake thundered after him, a sword in his hand. He shouted back over his shoulder, "Fools! I'll get him. Find those other brats!"

Tom ducked. Lord Mortlake ran past, his spurs ringing each time they hit the paving stones. Tom heard him clattering up the steps to the bell tower.

I have to warn Sebastian!

Tom ran through the hedged archway into the garden. The battle surged around him, but he stumbled on till he reached the shelter of the old oak tree. He looked up at the bell tower. Sebastian was hauling something up the wall.

"Sebastian!" Tom shouted. "Watch out!"

His friend did not hear him. He was concentrating hard, arm muscles bulging as he pulled on the heavy chain. The sun lit his curly hair to a fiery nimbus.

The next moment, Sebastian lifted up the heavy iron cage. Beltaine was crammed inside, the bars cutting into her wings. Tom also saw that Lord Mortlake had reached the floor below Sebastian and was climbing fast.

"Sebastian!" Tom's voice was croaky and did not make much noise. He tried again.

The squire unlocked the cage and lifted the baby dragon out. Beltaine burst into flight, looping around Sebastian's head. Tom saw Lord Mortlake sprinting up the stairs. He was almost upon Sebastian.

Tom screamed his name at the top of his lungs. Sebastian heard and turned just in time. A huge grin broke out on his face and he waved his arm. Then he disappeared behind the battlements, just as Lord Mortlake reached the top of the stairs. The armored lord stopped, looking around for Sebastian.

A great cacophony filled the air. Sebastian had climbed the final set of steps to the belfry and was now ringing the warning bells. Tom punched the air in victory. The townsfolk would hear the bells and come to the castle's rescue. Tom's father would hear the bells and come too.

A shadow fell upon him.

Lady Mortlake stood behind him, a long obsidian knife in her hand. The great boar stood beside her, as big as an ox, his eyes glaring red, drool dripping from his jaws.

"Why will you not die?" Lady Mortlake complained.

Elanor heard the bells ring out and cheered. She looked up at the bell tower, shading her eyes from the glare of the setting sun, hoping to see Tom.

But it was Sebastian up there ringing the bells. She could see his red curls and the darting shape of the baby dragon against the crimson-streaked sky.

Elanor's father had followed her out and was issuing orders to his men-at-arms. Sir Kevyn found a leather sack of weapons lying near the stables and shouted to his men to come and seize them.

A neigh rent the air and Elanor spun around. Quickthorn cantered towards her, his black mane and tail flying. Elanor ran to meet him, throwing her arms around his neck and burying her face in his neck.

The bells jangled into silence. Elanor looked up at the bell tower, but could see nothing. It was black against the smoky red sky. Sebastian must be running back down to the inner ward. Elanor wondered if Tom was with him.

Suddenly, she heard a distant explosion. It came from the dungeons below her feet. The whole castle shook and giant ravens rose up from the towers in a storm of black wings that darkened the whole sky. Elanor staggered. She would have fallen if it wasn't for the unicorn by her side. "No! Mistress Mauldred must've escaped!"

18

TIME OF THE DARK MOON

Elanor's legs felt weak. She looked around for help. Every one of her father's men were fighting desperately, barely able to hold their own against the endless ranks of bog-men. Lord Vaughn could barely be seen for the black-armored knights that surrounded him. Mistress Ifanna was down on one knee, only just managing to keep her shield above her head. The skeleton horse reared, Lady Rhianwyn struggling in the grip of a dozen bog-men. Only Sir Geraint held his own, arrows whizzing from his bow into the crowd as he sought to save his friends.

Elanor was amazed and gladdened to see folk from the town below in the struggle—butchers in striped aprons, fishermen with nets, a brawny-armed woman striking out with a frying pan. They all fought hard, but were being beaten back by the sheer number of bog-men and the knights with their swords and maces.

The door to the kitchen was blown off its hinges. Mistress Mauldred appeared, her fist surrounded by a ball of fiery power. She struck out, and one of the castle men-of-arms went flying backward, hit the wall and then lay still.

Elanor vaulted onto Quickthorn's back. "We have to stop her!" She dug her heels into the unicorn's side and he sprang forward into a gallop, wielding his horn with deadly accuracy as they raced through the battle. Each time his horn pierced the skin of a bog-man, the leathery creature burst into flame. Soon the air was filled with swirling ashes.

Mistress Mauldred stormed, livid, out into the inner ward. She saw Elanor and made a sharp gesture. Lighting crashed down. If the unicorn had not leapt, Elanor would have been struck.

Quickthorn spun and slashed with his horn. Mistress Mauldred stumbled back, blood welling from a deep gash on her arm. She looked up, furious, and made another quick motion with her hand. Lightning stabbed down again. Quickthorn neighed and bounded away. The lightning hit a knight in his metal armor and sent him flying. Mistress Mauldred struck again. This time, the lightning missed Quickthorn and Elanor by only a hairbreadth. Elanor could smell the burn of it in the air and feel its sizzle on her skin.

She wheeled Quickthorn around and galloped through the inner ward as Mistress Mauldred struck out left and right. It seemed her fiery magic would further turn the battle against the castle folk. Elanor saw her father fighting desperately, backed into a corner. Arwen was beside him, but the old witch was thin and frail from her weeks in the dungeon and her staff had been broken. It looked as if she would fall down at any moment.

Then Elanor saw Quinn racing towards her. A great silver-and-black serpent was draped around her neck and she carried a glass jar.

Elanor drew Quickthorn up. "Like a ride?"

Quinn nodded. Elanor pulled her up onto the back

of the beast. "Is that . . . is that Sabre?" Elanor looked at the snake wrapped around Quinn's neck.

"Yes. Wilda had shrunk him as small as a sardine, but I made him grow again. The only thing is, I didn't have much magic left. He only grew this big."

"Wilda?"

"Yes." Quinn waved the jar. "I have her right here."

Elanor squinted to see, then laughed out loud. The hunchbacked old witch was inside the jar, no bigger than her thumb.

"Where are the boys?" Quinn asked.

Elanor frowned. "I don't know. I haven't seen them for hours."

Just then, the bells began to clash together loudly.

Sebastian had been fighting Lord Mortlake for a long time. His legs trembled and his sword arm screamed in pain. A red mist swam before his eyes.

His only advantage was that he was younger and

quicker than the iron-clad lord. He ducked and veered and swerved and rolled, grateful for the many hours of mob-ball training. Beltaine helped, swooping around Lord Mortlake's head and spitting fiery sparks at him.

Then Sebastian stumbled. Lord Mortlake heaved him backward and Sebastian fell over the parapet and onto the largest of the bells. As Sebastian scrabbled madly, trying to keep himself from sliding off and falling down into the dark spaces below him, the bell swayed and smashed against the other bells.

Groping out, one of Sebastian's hands caught hold of the bell rope. He swung from side to side, trying to catch his breath. The clangor of the bells rang in his ears, deafening him.

Sebastian ached all over, bruised and bloodied. But Lord Mortlake was relentless, slashing at him with his sword. Sebastian scrambled up onto the curve of the bell, keeping its brass weight between him and the furious knight.

To the west, the sun was little more than a melting blob of liquid gold on the sea. Sebastian thought of the awakened warriors turning to dust and turned to look back down at the castle.

It was then that he saw a large army galloping up the road, banners fluttering amid a cloud of fiery-red dust.

Sebastian groaned. "What now?"

Quickthorn was surrounded by bog-men on all sides, grabbing at the girls' legs and arms and trying to drag them free. Just then, a whiplash of lightning flicked over their heads. It hit the jar in Quinn's hands and smashed it into smithereens. Wilda tumbled down, down, down. As soon as she hit the ground, she rolled over and planted her witch's staff into the earth. At once, she began to grow rapidly. Her ancient face was contorted with rage.

"Uh-oh!" Quinn cried.

Elanor urged Quickthorn into a gallop. The unicorn sped through the battle, Elanor clinging to his black mane and Quinn clinging to her. The snake lifted its triangular head and hissed.

The sun was sliding down behind the castle walls.

"It's almost sunset," Quinn cried in despair. "Then it'll be the time of the dark moon. We have to stop them before they destroy us all!"

Tom felt for his dagger. It was gone. So too were his bow and arrows. He was without weapons.

The giant boar pawed the ground with one foot, digging a great furrow in the soil. His red eyes were fixed on Tom.

Lady Mortlake smiled. She feinted towards Tom with the black knife. He ducked away. She struck again. Tom stumbled backward.

She pressed him hard against the oak tree, her dagger against his throat. "The sun is setting, and then comes the dark moon," she whispered. "Then will be the time to kill you. Even a pot boy's blood can curse a king."

BELLS OF VICTORY

Sebastian bolted down the steps, Lord Mortlake close on his heels.

To Sebastian's dismay, he saw that the battle had swung against the awakened heroes. All four were on their knees, each trying to stave off the spears and swords of dozens of knights and bog-men. Sir Kevyn's men-at-arms and the townsfolk were doing their best, but it was clear they would soon be overwhelmed.

The sky was darkening as the sun sank down in a welter of bloody colors. Then Sebastian heard the high, clear call of the horn. Sir Geraint had it to his lips, blowing a desperate retreat. A wild sweet-scented wind sprang up. It whirled around the inner ward. Dust and smoke and ashes swirled into little whirlwinds that danced back and forth across the darkening sky.

To his despair, Sebastian felt the golden sword in his hand turn into a spray of fiery sparks that swirled away on the wind.

When the air cleared, the awakened heroes were gone, and with them the magical weapons the children had won with such difficulty. The skeletons had all fallen into heaps of old bones, their animating blue light snuffed out.

"It's sunset," Lord Mortlake exulted. "And you've lost."

He swung his sword. Sebastian could do nothing but duck and run. As he raced through the archway into the garden, he saw Tom backed against the oak tree. Lady Mortlake had him cornered, an obsidian knife to his throat.

Quickthorn was rearing and prancing, Elanor and Quinn on his back. Mistress Mauldred was smiling as she forced them back towards the tree with one well-placed lightning bolt after another. Wilda advanced from behind. Sebastian glanced over his shoulder. Lord Mortlake's sword gleamed in his hand as he stepped closer and closer, smiling ferociously.

"Your heroes are nothing but dust now," the lord gloated. "Your weapons are all broken and your protectors are dead. It is sunset, and the moon is dark. Now is the time to cast the death curse."

"All we need is blood." Mistress Mauldred drew a black blade from within her dress. She darted forward and seized Elanor's ankle, dragging her from the unicorn. Quickthorn reared, trying to protect her.

Quinn fell to the ground. As she painfully drew herself to her feet, Wilda darted forward and drew her own witch's knife. She dragged Quinn backward, holding her in front of her, the knife to her chest. Sabre coiled before them, rearing high and hissing his defiance, but unable to strike with Quinn between him and the witch.

"Ela!" Tom stretched out his hand in horror as Mistress Mauldred pressed her blade against Elanor's throat. He could not run to help her, though, for he was still pressed back to the tree, Lady Mortlake's knife sharp and cruel against his skin. He could feel blood sliding down his skin. She laughed and pressed the blade closer.

An eagle's scream split the twilight sky. A magnificent golden griffin swooped down and landed in the garden. He could do nothing to save Tom, though, and his long lion's tail thrashed in angry frustration.

Sebastian was backed closer and closer to the tree by the point of Lord Mortlake's sword. "How much more satisfying it will be to kill you myself," the lord said. "And with the death of the four of you, we shall rid ourselves of all who stand between us and the throne."

Beltaine swooped around Lord Mortlake's head, desperately, spraying fiery sparks. Lord Mortlake simply swatted her away with his gauntleted fist. Whimpering, the baby dragon spun away, head over heels, then crashed to the ground. "Bel!" Sebastian cried, but he could do nothing.

All four children were backed against the oak tree, blades at their throats.

"Start the spell!" Mistress Mauldred commanded.

Lady Mortlake laughed. "*By the power of the dark moon, with bloodied corpses of battle here strewn . . .*" the witch chanted. As the blade cut deeper, Tom felt the trickle of his blood flow faster.

". . . *with the shedding of royal blood, I open Death's dark flood . . .*" Mistress Mauldred pressed the dagger into Elanor's throat. Blood streaked down her pale skin. Lord Mortlake smiled and pressed the point of his sword into Sebastian's shoulder so he gasped with pain. Wilda grinned toothlessly and began twisting the blade above Quinn's heart so blood bloomed on her white dress.

"Stop!" a voice commanded.

Arwen limped into the shadowed circle under the oak tree's ancient branches. "Kill me instead," she begged. "I am old, and these brave children are so young . . ."

"A Grand Teller's blood will make powerful death magic indeed," Lady Mortlake cried. With a scream of triumph, she leapt forward and plunged her dagger into Arwen's breast. The silver-haired witch fell, her blood spilling out to stain the churned mud.

"*With this willing sacrifice . . .*" Mistress Mauldred began to chant.

"No!" Quinn screamed. She pushed Wilda away and stumbled towards the fallen body of the Grand Teller. Wilda fell down to her knees, rats scuttling away. The serpent raised high his flat head, swaying at the end of his long, sinuous neck. He hissed in warning and the old witch shrank in fear.

Quinn bent over the crumpled body of her teacher. One hand sought the wooden medallion around her neck. "Oh what can I do, what can I do?"

A deep voice boomed out. "Hast thou forgotten thy gifts? Thou hast what thou needst within thee, as an acorn carries a forest in its heart."

Sebastian jerked in surprise. It was the Oak King's voice, he was sure of it. He had never heard Sylvan speak before, though Elanor had. He put up one hand to the wooden dragon brooch that had been Arwen's gift to him. Lord Mortlake was angrily looking around for the source of the voice and not paying any attention to the boy he held at sword-point. Sebastian unhooked the brooch from his cloak and drove the sharp pin deep into Lord Mortlake's shoulder. He roared in pain and surprise and staggered backward, one hand clapped to the wound. At once, Beltaine swooped down and blasted him with fire, turning his iron breastplate a sullen red. Lord Mortlake staggered back, dropping his sword.

At the exact same moment, Elanor lifted her hand to her mouth and blew upon her ring. A crackling blue shield of energy leapt up between her and Mistress Mauldred, knocking the witch backward, head over heels. At once, Quickthorn leapt forward and stood before Elanor, guarding her as Lady Mortlake rushed to help her sister.

Tom was left unguarded. He slipped one hand inside his shirt and drew out the battered wooden flute that Arwen had given him, putting it to his lips. He blew one long tremulous note.

"You think to enchant me with your little flute?" Lady Mortlake turned back to face him. The ring on her left hand was glowing red. "A child like you? Why, you're nothing but a pot boy."

Tom's tune faltered.

Lady Mortlake smiled. "You think to be a hero, but it's only a silly childish dream. *Wake up, child.* A pot boy you were born and a pot boy you'll remain."

His throat muscles had constricted so much Tom could not take a breath to blow into the flute. His hands lowered. His vision blurred.

"Don't listen to her!" Elanor called.

"Don't stop, Tom!" Quinn called, her voice breaking with tears. "You can be whatever you want! No one can choose our lives for us!"

Sebastian shouted, "Tom, you're the bravest hero of us all! Don't listen!"

"Pot boy," Lady Mortlake taunted, striding back towards him, her knife held ready.

Tom hung his head.

Lady Mortlake stepped closer, her knife held high. Tom sidled away, looking from side to side. His back bumped against the oak tree. He put one hand upon it, feeling the rough, fissured bark against his fingertips.

"It is all within thee, like an orchard inside an apple seed," the Oak King boomed, his deep voice echoing around the twilight glade.

The Grand Teller lifted her head. Her voice sounded in Tom's mind: *If you are brave of heart, sharp of wit, strong of spirit and steadfast of purpose, there is nothing you cannot achieve . . .*

Tom took a deep breath, lifted the flute to his mouth again and began to play with all his might. The notes were deep and strong and shook with power. The Oak King began to sing:

"DARK MOON, I CALL TO THEE,
DYING SUN, I CALL TO THEE,
RISING STARS, I CALL TO THEE,
IT IS TIME, IT IS TIME, IT IS TIME.
CRACKER OF STONES, I CALL TO THEE,
BLOSSOMS OF BONE, I CALL TO THEE,
SEEDS THAT HAVE BEEN SOWN, I CALL TO THEE,
IT IS TIME, IT IS TIME, IT IS TIME."

The Oak King's voice quickened and rose, and Tom's flute playing echoed him, the tune spiraling out into the twilight garden.

"IT IS TIME TO RISE,

ALL THEE THAT ARE GREEN AND GROWING,

IT IS TIME TO RISE,

ALL THEE THAT ARE BLUE AND BLOWING,

IT IS TIME TO RISE,

ALL THEE THAT ARE GOLDEN AND GLOWING,

IT IS TIME TO RISE,

ALL THEE THAT ARE RED AND HARROWING."

High and wild and sweet, the flute music spiraled up towards the stars, now blazing out in a violet-blue sky. The wind whirled through the garden, blowing away all the smoke and ashes, and making Elanor's hair stream out like a silken banner. The trees in the sacred circle all bent and creaked, the whispering of their leaves making a song of their own. Sparks flew past like tiny flaming beetles.

Sebastian felt as though he was rooted into the ground. He saw that all the others were as still, their bodies bent in the shape they had been in when the song begun. There was terror on Wilda's wrinkled face and Lord Mortlake's lips were drawn back from his teeth in a snarl of rage. The two witch sisters clung together, their eyes dark with dread.

Then the trees lurched and swayed, their branches reaching out like great clawed hands. Brambles and briars sprung up around the feet of the four villains, weaving together faster than the eye could follow.

"It is time to pay for thy evil deeds," the Oak King said, his voice hoarse with exhaustion. "It is time to reap the harvest thou hast sown."

For a moment, all was quiet. Lord Mortlake and his accomplices were all imprisoned within cages woven of twigs and thorns. The scene was lit by dancing fireflies. Sebastian saw that fierce-faced faeries rode on their backs, holding tiny blowpipes made of angelica stalks.

"Let us out!" Lord Mortlake shook the wooden bars of his cage.

"You'll pay for this!" his wife screamed.

"I order you to release me." Mistress Mauldred shook her finger at Elanor.

"Please help me," Wilda whimpered. "I'm just a poor old woman. I never meant any harm."

The children all started talking at once.

"We did it!" Sebastian and Elanor grasped each other's hands, and jumped up and down in excitement.

"Thank you, Sylvan." Quinn cupped one hand around the wooden medallion.

"Have you ever heard such music?" Tom said wonderingly. He rubbed the wooden flute lovingly.

"Look to the lady," the Oak King said, in a voice so raspy and tired it was hard to understand. "Her life blood is ebbing away."

Elanor ran to where Arwen lay crumpled on the grass. The old witch's eyes were closed, the skin around her mouth blue. Her white robe was stained with blood. Elanor dragged out the stopper of her water bottle and then bent to pour the last drops of the enchanted water into the old witch's slack mouth.

For a moment, nothing happened. Then Arwen coughed, and lifted one frail hand. The unicorn pranced over and laid his sharp horn against the deep wound in her breast. The blood shrank away, and the flesh closed. Arwen smiled.

"Lift me up," she whispered. "I want to dance."

Music had begun to fill the dark garden once

again. The deep, rhythmic beating of a drum, the infectious call of a fiddle, the sweet notes of a lap harp. Tom turned and saw, to his utter amazement, that the crooked old elder tree at the far end of the garden had split open and a whole host of faery folk were dancing out into the gloaming. Leading the way was an old, old woman, dressed in a cloak of leaves with a crown made of elderberries on her silvery-white hair. She lifted her skirt and pointed her toe and danced forward, smiling. Around her head spun a halo of tiny, shining faeries, their wings like stars. A short, fat, bearded man in a brown coat and a red hat danced a jig behind her. More of the Ellyllon zoomed past, riding on the backs of iridescent winged beetles. A group of tall, fair-haired elves waltzed past, their clothes made of spider silk and flower petals. Dark-skinned brownies tumbled around, turning cartwheels and backflips.

Many were playing instruments. Filled with wonder, Tom lifted his flute to his mouth and played as he had never played before.

People came dancing through the trees. Knights in black armor. Bakers in tall white hats, waving rolling pins. Women in aprons and clogs, with frying pans in their hands. They all danced into the green garth, laughing and calling to Tom.

Lord Wolfgang danced past, holding the hand of Sophie the kitchen maid. Sabre swayed back and forth, eyes slitted in pleasure. Beltaine did a somersault, spitting circles of fiery sparks like fireworks. Quickthorn pranced and bowed his horned head to Rex, who spread his wings and lashed his tail.

Then the old woman in the crown of elderberries began to sing and all the faeries joined in. Their voices were high and wild and sweet, and their song echoed from every stone till it seemed as if the castle itself had broken into song.

And the stones of the castle sing . . .

The bells rang out, pealing joyously.

And the bells of victory ring . . .

Tom could play no longer. The moment overwhelmed him. All around him people sang and danced and laughed. Tom looked around him in awe. Was it true? Had they won? Was it possible?

Grinning, Sebastian raced to hug Tom. "You did

it! To think all those hours of fighting couldn't defeat them and you did it with a song."

Elanor and Quinn were leaping joyfully with Arwen, who looked more spry than she had for years. Tom and Sebastian raced to join them, laughing as they saw their beasts celebrating in their own wild ways. Beltaine and Rex were swooping high in the starlit sky, while Quickthorn was prancing with a dozen tiny faeries spinning around his horned head. Sabre was swaying back and forth, his long body coiled below him. Somewhere, far above, bats and ravens wheeled and whirled.

The four friends held hands and spun around, unable to believe that they had, in the end, triumphed.

"Tom, you're a hero!" Elanor cried.

He laughed. "We're all heroes, Ela! To think I thought that flute was useless!"

"Can you believe it? We did it!" Quinn cried.

"I always knew we would!" Sebastian said.

20

A Truly Impossible Quest

An army of knights galloped into the inner ward. "Valor, glory, victory!" a huge voice bellowed.

Sebastian stepped forward with a disbelieving laugh. "Too late, Father!"

The leader of the army pulled off his golden helmet. "What?!" he exclaimed. "I was hoping for a nice, bloody fight. Are we really too late?"

Sebastian indicated the four villains, lying bound at his feet. "We wrapped up without you."

Lord Byrne slumped in disappointment.

"But we could probably rustle you up a feast," Sebastian said.

His father perked up. "A feast?"

Sebastian pointed. "The kitchen's that way, Father. See what you can find for us. I'm starving."

Then Tom heard a much-beloved voice. "Tomkin!"

He looked around eagerly. There was his mother. Her hair was a bird's nest, her face was streaked with dirt and she was considerably thinner, but she flung open her arms in her usual loving way, and Tom went into them like an arrow into the gold. He could not speak. Nor could she. They just hugged.

A howling pierced the night. Tom saw a tall, shaggy shape striding through the dancing crowd. It was his father, surrounded by wolves.

"Hunter!" his mother cried. She seized Tom's hand and they ran towards him. Then Tom saw, with a joyful bound of his heart, that his wolfhound Fergus sat amongst the wolves, howling away jubilantly with them. Between his forelegs crouched a fluff ball of wolf cub, his muzzle pointed up at the stars.

"Fergus!" Tom flung himself down on his knees, hugging his wolfhound. Then he gathered Wulfric into his arms. "Where have you been?"

"They came to find me," Tom's father said.

Tom looked up. Hunter stood with both arms clasped firmly around Tom's mother's waist. He did not seem to mind her bird's nest hair and she did not seem to mind his shaggy wolf-skin clothes.

"I came as fast as I could," Hunter went on. "We had some fierce fighting with Lord Mortlake's border guards. But we got here in the end."

"That's all that counts." Tom's mother snuggled her arms tighter around him.

Tom felt a bubble of happiness inside him.

Hunter smiled and drew off the ring he wore on his finger. "Will you take back your ring?"

Tom's mother put both hands on her hips. "Will you come live in the castle like an ordinary man?"

Hunter looked uncomfortable. "Perhaps, if Lord Wolfgang promises to stop killing the wolves."

"I think Lord Wolfgang has had enough of killing to last a lifetime," she answered dryly.

"Well then, maybe . . . in the winter, at least."

When his father bent his head to kiss his mother, Tom slipped away into the darkness, the wolfhound and the wolf at his heels.

Kissing was all well and good, but he did not want to watch it.

Sebastian's father had somehow managed to assemble a feast of epic proportions. The four children were starving, and they gathered around the table, talking around mouthfuls of fresh white bread crammed with roast pheasant and red currant jelly.

"How did you get here so fast?" Sebastian asked his father. "We thought we wouldn't see you for days."

Lord Byrne grinned. "Your mother was worried about you. We were getting these long, gushing letters about how good it was here. Not a spelling mistake in sight! We knew something was wrong."

Sebastian laughed till he almost cried. Quinn, Elanor and Tom laughed with him.

Then Jack rushed up, dressed in a shining suit of chain mail that was rather too big for her. She had found Lord Byrne only half a day's ride away, she told them, and he had galloped the rest of the way. "He was beside himself with worry for you," she told Sebastian.

Lord Byrne went bright red. "Well, you can't blame a father for being worried about his son, can you? Not that there was any need, I can see. You handled that blighter Lord Mortlake on your own. Told your mother, I did. Sebastian can look after himself."

Sebastian's grin had never been so wide.

"There's only one thing that worries me," Quinn said. "What happened to the four warriors? Did they retreat to the hidden chamber in time?"

"I heard them call the retreat," Sebastian said. "And my sword just dissolved in my hand."

"I hope they are back under the castle," Elanor said. "Waiting till they are needed again."

For a moment, all four were quiet.

"The strange thing is," Quinn said, "some people are saying they saw the legendary heroes ride . . ."

"And others think it was us," Sebastian added, looking very pleased about it all.

"Father wants to knight you," Elanor told Tom.

"But I thought you'd rather be trained to be a

minstrel," Quinn said. She added, with a shy smile, "Who knows, maybe one day you could be the Grand Minstrel at the royal court?"

Tom stared at her, unable to speak for the sudden hope in his chest.

"The thing is," Elanor said in a burst, "Father cannot seek justice on his own. What the Mortlakes did was treason. He has to take them all to Stormness to seek the king's justice. He wants us all to go, too, so the king can thank us."

"I should probably go anyway," Quinn said. "Since the king is meant to be my great-uncle."

"You mean to claim your throne," Tom breathed.

Quinn smiled at him and shrugged, spreading wide her hands. "I don't know. Maybe."

Sebastian grinned. "Now that truly would be an impossible quest."

They all laughed, knowing that none of them believed anything was impossible anymore.